MY FATE ACCORDING to the BUTTERFLY

MY
FATE
ACCORDING
to the
BUTTERFLY

by
GAIL D.
VILLANUEVA

SCHOLASTIC PRESS
NEW YORK

Library of Congress Cataloging-in-Publication Data
Names: Villanueva, Gail D., author.
Title: My fate according to the butterfly / by Gail D. Villanueva.
Description: First edition. | New York: Scholastic Press, 2019. | Summary:
    In one week Sabrina will be eleven-years-old and she would really like to
    get her estranged parents and her older sister Nadine together for the
    celebration, especially since the black butterfly landing on her locket
    has convinced her that she is going to die; Sabrina and her friend Pepper
    come up with a bucket list, and enlist Nadine's help—but aspiring
    reporter Nadine is working on a story about the Philippines' war on drugs,
    and she has uncovered something that may endanger them all, and prove the
    butterfly is indeed a harbinger of death in Manila.
Identifiers: LCCN 2018046396 (print) | LCCN 2018058288 (ebook) | ISBN 9781338310528 |
    ISBN 9781338310504 (hardcover)
Subjects: LCSH: Superstition—Juvenile fiction. | Drug
    traffic—Philippines—Manila—Juvenile fiction. | Reporters and
    reporting—Philippines—Manila—Juvenile fiction. | Sisters—Juvenile
    fiction. | Families—Philippines—Manila—Juvenile fiction. | Parent and
    child—Juvenile fiction. | Manila (Philippines)—Juvenile fiction. | CYAC:
    Superstition—Fiction. | Drug traffic—Fiction. | Reporters and
    reporting—Fiction. | Sisters—Fiction. | Family life—Philippines—
    Manila—Fiction. | Parent and child—Fiction. | Manila (Philippines)—
    Fiction. | Philippines—Fiction.
Classification: LCC PZ7.1.V54 (ebook) | LCC PZ7.1.V54 My 2019 (print) |
    DDC [Fic]—dc23

10 9 8 7 6 5 4 3 2 1   19 20 21 22 23

Printed in the U.S.A.   37
First edition, August 2019
Book design by Baily Crawford

IF YOU'RE SEARCHING FOR A WINDOW TO LOOK THROUGH,
OR YEARNING FOR A MIRROR TO SEE YOURSELF IN,
THIS BOOK IS FOR YOU.

CHAPTER ONE

An Utterly Impossible Task

SUNDAY

IF YOU SEE THE BUTTERFLY, somebody you know will die.

Or has already died. My dad wasn't clear. He just said if the Butterfly lands on something of yours, you should expect Death to come knocking at your door.

"Butterflies again?"

That's my *ate*, my big sister, Nadine. She doesn't believe in the Butterfly.

Well, Ate Nadine doesn't believe *anything* Dad says.

"You've got this entire park to inspire you, and you pick those pesky little things," she continues, sitting beside me. Ate Nadine tosses her silver notebook on the picnic table. "I swear, Sab. This obsession needs to stop."

It's a little after one in the afternoon—the time of the day when the humid, sweltering heat of Metro Manila is most unforgiving. Ate Nadine and I are wearing similar tank tops and denim shorts, but hers look fresh and clean. Mine, on the other hand, are icky with sweat and smeared with oil pastel.

"I'm not obsessed." I flip my painting over, hiding it from her sight.

Thing is, I do love to draw and paint butterflies. But I never color them black, nor do I make them bigger than an inch or two. Okay, maybe I *am* obsessed with drawing other kinds of butterflies, since I can't bring myself to draw *the* Butterfly.

Dad described the Butterfly as being as black as a starless night sky. It's a giant compared to your garden-variety moth— probably even bigger than my hand. Its dark, mysterious vibe is beautiful and sinister at the same time. A perfect inspiration for a newbie artist like me.

Still, I can't get myself to create anything remotely resembling my father's Butterfly. Call me superstitious, but no way am I making art that might bring bad luck to our family.

"Stop being so melodramatic. It's not like I can't un-flip your painting." Ate Nadine rolls her eyes. "Let me see."

I study my sister. We have the same bronze skin, flat nose, and small, dark brown eyes. But her black hair cascades on her shoulders in soft waves, and mine hangs from my head like a dull wig. I have skinny arms, and she has curves. During my insecure moments, I think of her as an upgraded version of me. On days like this one, however, I look up to Ate Nadine.

I'm pretty sure I managed to capture the view of a bug from the ground. Still, I want to know my sister's opinion, so I push the artwork across the table.

"It's fine, but you need to add more shadows behind the blades of grass. Right now, it looks like a picture frame of fake leaves," Ate Nadine says in a brisk manner. She's harsh, but I'll take it. I'm lucky she has time to look at my work at all.

Ever since my sister went off to college and started writing for the school paper, I barely see her. She often comes home late on school nights. On weekends she's cooped up in her room with the music blasting so loud the floor vibrates in the hallway. When I *do* see Ate Nadine, she's either typing away on her laptop or bickering with someone on the phone.

I thought she'd have time for me now, since it's summer. Then Ate Nadine got this internship with a national paper, and it just got worse.

"I love how you blended the blue hues for the sky here," she continues. "The butterflies' colors pop out nicely, but if you put more—"

"I think it's pretty," says a chirpy voice behind me. I look over my shoulder and find myself staring at the bright blue eyes of my best friend, Pepper Lemmington. "I love the details on those butterflies. You make them look so real."

Ate Nadine snorts. "You think everything Sab paints is pretty."

I beam at my friend. If Ate Nadine is my harshest critic, Pepper is my greatest cheerleader. She's been my best friend since first grade, when she and her dad moved permanently to the Philippines from the United States.

"True." Pepper shrugs. "Still—"

CREEENG!

There's a loud ring coming from Ate Nadine's shorts pocket. She hands me back my work and answers her cell phone. "Hello? Yes, this is she. You mean the one that went viral? Yes, ma'am, I wrote it. Uh-huh . . ."

So much for my art critique. Whenever her internship mentor calls, Ate drops everything, including me.

She's right though. The lighting and shadows on my painting do need fixing.

I smooth down the edges of my artwork. The oil pastels leave green-and-blue smudges on my fingers, as well as a distinct smell I find most comforting. Waxy, but with a hint of something like face powder. I create a thin black outline beneath a leaf and use the tip of my index finger to blend it in.

"Nice." Pepper nods in approval. "It's so much better now."

"Ahh-teh Nah-deen!" I call, waving my painting like a flag to catch my sister's attention. "I'm done. What do you think?"

"I don't think they get it on campus, but the main distributor is definitely nearby. Uh-huh. Maybe. There aren't any famous politicians who went to San Jose Pignatelli College. The school would publicize it if someone did. Yes, I understand. A byline? Oh my g— Yes, ma'am. I'll find as much evidence as

I can. You can count on me," Ate Nadine says to the person on the phone. As Nadine stands up she throws me a look so deadly I jump and knock my things off the table.

"She's just busy." Pepper helps me put the oil pastels back into the box. I avoid her gaze, but I can feel the pity in her eyes. "I'm sure Ate Nadine will make it up to you on your birthday."

"I doubt she'll even remember." I say it more roughly than I intend to.

Mom's in Singapore for a conference, and there's a chance she won't make it back in time for my eleventh birthday next Sunday. I thought it would be okay. Mom's boyfriend is taking care of us, and Ate Nadine has to keep Pepper and me company while he's at work.

Kind of like today. But even though Ate Nadine's just a few feet away, her mind is obviously elsewhere.

"I wish Dad were here." I stuff the wax-crayon case in my backpack, zipping it closed. "He's weird, but at least he's fun."

Ate Nadine continues to pace under the mango tree with the phone on her ear. I try to hear what she's saying, but the words mean nothing to me.

"Come on." Pepper glances at the park entrance. Nannies and dog walkers are coming in for afternoon playtime. Pepper and I quicken our steps. We claim the swings at the corner of the park before anyone else does.

I hold the chains tightly, balancing myself on the hanging seat. My breath goes out in quick intervals, almost as fast as the thumping in my chest. I'm on the brink of an asthma attack.

Pepper clucks her tongue and reaches behind me. From my backpack, she brings out the inhaler, which I grab with shaking fingers. I press the metal canister, spraying medicine into my mouth. It leaves a bitter aftertaste, but it stops my asthma from going any further.

"You should keep that thing near," my friend says, helping me wiggle out of the backpack. She zips it closed and tosses it on the grass. "Chill out, Sab. It's your birthday next week. If I were the one turning eleven, I'd be more excited."

Easy for her to say. Pepper has her family to celebrate it with—my own mom probably can't even make it to mine. And now, I wouldn't be surprised if my sister won't be able to either.

"What do you want to do for your birthday anyway? We can start planning it!" Pepper kicks at the ground and swings, her brown hair trailing behind her.

Pepper could have a career as a tween model if she wanted to—girls who have a light complexion usually do. With her blue eyes and creamy-white skin, she's the most beautiful ten-year-old I know.

Ate Nadine said that I think of Pepper this way because I'm a product of colonial mentality. "When Spain colonized the Philippines, they made sure we remember they're better than we are. They had this whole tax system where rich white Spaniards paid little. We paid more even though we did more of the work, just because we're brown," she explained. "Our American colonizers weren't any better. Sure, we got more rights and education and all that. But the mentality remained the same—white is beautiful, brown is not."

My sister tends to sound like a boring history book if you make the mistake of asking her to explain something. I just know my friend's pretty, prettier than I'll ever dream to be.

My hand reaches for the locket on my chest as I start to answer Pepper, but I grasp air instead. I never take the locket off except to shower—I can't believe I forgot to put it back on this morning. It was from Dad. Unlike Ate Nadine, I value his gifts and actually use them. I let out a long sigh. "Birthday brunch at Lola Cordia's Garden Resort would be great."

Pepper stops swinging. "Your dead grandma's resort? The one your papa inherited?"

"Yeah." I wince. Maybe it's a cultural thing, that Pepper's more blunt and honest than any of my Filipino classmates. So, I just try to understand her.

"Your papa's there. *And* Wendell. Ate Nadine—"

"I know." I follow her lead and slow down my swing. Ate Nadine would rather drop dead than spend a second in Dad's company. But Pepper's brilliant. Nothing is impossible with her. "Can you come up with a plan to get Ate Nadine to come?"

"That's a tall order, Sab. Your sister's really stubborn." Pepper takes a lock of her brown hair and twirls it around a finger. "Don't worry. I'll think of something."

Great.

Pepper's biting her lower lip. I don't see her do that often, but when I do, it worries me. Because it almost always means she's worried too.

I force myself to smile as my sister heads our way. If Pepper isn't sure she can come up with a plan, I might as well accept this birthday reunion isn't happening. Ate Nadine will never speak to Dad, and that's just the way it is.

CHAPTER TWO
Beware the Shark

PEPPER GOES HOME BEFORE DINNER, but she leaves me with an assignment.

"Test the waters," she says. "Ate Nadine's in a good mood. Maybe she'll agree to talk to your papa."

Easy for Pepper to say. It'll be like dipping my toe in a tank full of sharks, and I can't do this alone. I need reinforcements. I need my pet Pekin duck, Lawin.

Lawin is the Filipino word for "hawk." It's like naming a cute little puppy "Wolf"—a name too intimidating for its holder. But Lawin is a brave little guy; he totally deserves his name.

I wish that some of Lawin's courage could rub off on me right now.

As expected, my sister's in her room, busy typing at her laptop. Her fingers dance over the keys so fast it's a wonder she's able to get anything down correctly. I can't even type my own name without struggling to find where the letters are.

Sometimes I complain a lot about my sister's busy schedule, but I'm proud of her. She's always been great with words, unlike me. I had trouble learning to read, and I would have taken even longer had it not been for Ate Nadine. Mom tutored me whenever she had time off from work. But it was my sister who taught me how to make sense of those groups of letters. She painted flash cards that helped me associate words with pictures.

I wish I had Ate Nadine's way with words so I could convince her that we should spend my birthday weekend with Dad.

"Ate."

My sister's brows furrow in concentration as she continues to type on her keyboard, glancing at her silver journal every now and then.

"Ahh-tehh!"

"Don't shout, Sab." Ate Nadine finally looks up from her computer, glaring at me. "And get that ugly duck off my rug before he poops."

"He's not ugly." Actually, he is, but I don't want him to hear her say so. At five weeks old, Lawin's no longer the cute duckling he was when Pepper first gave him to me. His yellow fuzz is coming off as white feathers begin to emerge. Almost everything about him has grown five times in size—head, body, and even his feet. His wings, on the other hand, remain tiny.

Lawin resembles the creature you'd get if you crossed a platypus, a raptor, and a half-plucked chicken. It's a terrible combination. He's at the stage where he's not quite a teenager but no longer a baby either. Kind of like me.

But I'm not here to argue with Ate Nadine about Lawin. I take a deep breath. *Test the waters. I can do this.* "I thought about Dad today."

Ate Nadine's fingers freeze in midtype, and her back stiffens. "So?"

"Well," I begin, shifting my feet. *Come on, self. Just dip your toe in before the shark bites.* "I was thinking . . . It's my birthday next week, and it's been a year since you've last seen Dad—"

Ate Nadine turns, her eyes staring at me like laser beams. I want to open a hole in the floor and have it swallow me whole.

"What do you want, Sab?"

"Uhm . . ." I want to spend my birthday at Dad's resort. I want Mommy to come home. I want Ate Nadine and Daddy to set aside whatever issue they have so we can be a family again. I want to say all these things, but I'm having trouble getting the words to form. It's like a part of me wants to be brave, but another part is so scared that it's refusing to let my brain know what to say.

As I muster courage, there's a distant ringing.

"Answer the phone downstairs," Ate Nadine orders, her voice rough. "I'm working."

I can't believe I just threw away my chance to ask. "But—"

"*Now*, Sab."

Defeated, I grab Lawin and hurry to Mom's office. I tested the waters, got bitten by the shark, and failed.

"Sabrina?" a man says from the other end of the line. It's my dad's boyfriend, Wendell. His voice is high-pitched and squeaky, quite like how you'd imagine a tiny elf's voice to be. "Is that you? Are you okay? How about your sister?"

Lawin waddles around the room, then settles near my feet. Careful not to disturb the resting duck, I take a pencil from the holder and pull a notepad in front of me. I draw two circles and two cylinders, filling in the details so they look human.

"Hi, Wendell. We're fine."

Unlike my parents' Filipino friends, Wendell doesn't want my sister and me to refer to him as *uncle*. Aside from being much younger than our parents, Wendell grew up in the United States. His Filipina mom died when he was a baby, so he was brought up by his Italian American dad. He might have mastered the art of pasta making, but there really wasn't anyone who could teach him about Filipino titles.

Still, Wendell's been in the Philippines for ten years already. He's spent a lot of time running the family resort, first as Lola Cordia's assistant and now the manager. Wendell interacts a lot with the staff. I guess getting called "Tito Wendell" is just too strange for him. Ate Nadine said it's because Wendell doesn't like the idea of being referred to as Dad's brother instead of his boyfriend.

Wendell breathes a sigh of relief, and his mouthpiece amplifies the sound. I wince, but I keep the phone to my ear. The pencil in my left hand continues to slide over the paper. I finish the last touches on my doodle—two men holding hands.

"Your dad won't stop hounding me about you girls," says Wendell. "We haven't heard from you in a while. You know how your dad gets after working on a new piece."

Oh, I do.

Dad's concentration is so intense when he's working on a sculpture. I wouldn't be surprised if he forgets he has children, or even knows he's on planet earth. Still, when Dad emerges from his artistic trances, he's fun to be with. We had these art sessions where he'd teach Ate Nadine and me something new like calligraphy or Chinese painting.

Come to think of it, Dad did seem like he was elsewhere most of the time. But Wendell can tolerate Dad's "space cadet" moments, even at times when Mom and Ate Nadine couldn't. I guess that's why he and Dad are together.

"Anyway . . ." Wendell clears his throat. "We'd really love to have you and Nadine visit us here at the resort. We were even thinking . . . You could celebrate your birthday here!"

Funny. It's almost as if Wendell read my mind.

"I'll order a roast pig and all the ice cream flavors you want. Bring Pepper and your mom too! Is she still with the police guy?"

"Yeah, Mom and Tito Ed are still together." My forehead creases in a frown. I tear the drawing off the notepad and crumple it into a ball.

Tito Ed isn't really my tito either. He's my mother's

boyfriend. They've been together for three years, but Mom and Tito Ed can't get married because divorce isn't allowed in the Philippines. Mom and Dad's only options, legal separation or annulment, are too complicated.

I've always considered Wendell "Dad Number Two" and Tito Ed "Dad Number Three." It's not something I tell anyone without being asked. Awkward pauses usually follow my explanations. Still, the three of them—Dad, Wendell, and Tito Ed—care for Ate Nadine and me in their own fatherly ways. They all deserve to be called Dad.

I thought Ate Nadine felt the same way. I remember this one instance when Dad was getting treatment from that purple-and-pink building in Pasig. It didn't look like a hospital at all, more like a school. Mom told us Dad had a medical condition, so he needed to stay there for a while. Ate Nadine looked like she couldn't bear to leave Dad, crying all the way home.

Then my grandma, Lola Cordia, died last year, and everything changed. My sister never said why.

Wendell is still talking about all the fun things we could do if we came to the resort, but if my pathetic attempt at "testing the waters" was any indication, there's no way Ate Nadine would go for it. Even if the food spread does sound like heaven.

I aim for the wastebasket across the room, throw the crumpled paper like a basketball, and miss. "Ate Nadine will never agree to it."

"I'm sorry." Wendell sighs again. I'm getting used to hearing air blown into the mouthpiece, so I don't wince this time. "Your dad talks about you and Nadine a lot, you know. Not a day goes by that he doesn't mention your names. He really misses you—both of you."

"I'll see what I can do about going there," I promise, even though I know it's a lost cause. Because really, what *can* I do? I tried to ask but chickened out—which is probably all for the best. What if Ate Nadine had gotten mad at me? I would spend my eleventh birthday not only Mom-less, but sister-less too. I wish I knew why she stopped speaking to Dad. But no one has ever told me what happened. "Ate is so stubborn."

"I know." Wendell chortles. It's high-pitched, like Minnie Mouse's giggle, but comforting somehow. "Well, let us know if there's anything we can do to help. And, Sab? Tell Nadine that your dad . . ."

"Yes?"

Wendell pauses. "Just tell her to give me a call, will you? See you soon."

There's a beep when Wendell hangs up, and I place the phone receiver back in its cradle.

Ate Nadine doesn't mind talking to Wendell. But he should know better than to discuss Dad with my sister.

I glance at the desk clock—it's almost five. The afternoon sun has turned the sterile white walls of Mom's office orange. It's so bright it's hard to see the shed in the garden. It's hard to see anything outside, for that matter.

Nightfall's coming.

"Wake up, Lawin." Sighing, I walk across the room to clean up the crumpled paper mess I made on the floor. The duck stares at me with a beady eye as he stretches his legs.

Pepper and I still don't have a plan. I'm not even sure there will be one. If *only* there was a way to get Ate Nadine to work things out with our father, to take me to the resort for my birthday . . .

As I stand, my gaze falls on the shelf where Mom displays photos of our family. They're mostly of Ate Nadine, Mom, Tito Ed, and me. Some are of Mom's parents; a few are of my lolo and lola on Dad's side.

My favorite is this family photo, the last one we had with my grandmother. It shows my sister, our parents, Tito Ed,

Wendell, Lola Cordia, and me smiling at the camera. Behind us is a background of blue, green, and yellow blots. It's a blurred image of the sky and ylang-ylang trees around my grandmother's beloved butterfly garden. The day we had the photo taken was the same as today—a humid March summer afternoon.

"Oh!" I cry. Next to the photo on the shelf is a silver locket—my locket. I must have left it on the shelf when I talked to Mom this morning, right after taking a shower.

A breeze enters the room, smelling like grass and ripe mangoes. But it also brings in a shower of dust as it passes through Mom's old books and journals. Lawin lets out a series of quacks, running around in circles as he frantically flaps his wings.

"Ah-choo!" I rub my eyes once to relieve the itch, blinking as they begin to water. That's when I see it fluttering into the room—a huge pitch-black butterfly.

The Butterfly.

The one Dad warned me about. I'm sure of it.

My pulse quickens, and goose bumps appear on my arms. I get a sick feeling in my stomach as I remember the stories Dad used to tell me. How the Butterfly appeared days before his cousin drowned. How it warned Dad of a friend's death before she succumbed to cancer. How Dad listened to Lola Cordia cry herself to sleep after the Butterfly showed her that it was her husband's turn to die.

"Oh no." My hands turn clammy and cold. This can't be happening. "No, no, no."

I want to shoo the Butterfly away, but I'm too afraid to touch it.

I hold my breath as the Butterfly hovers above the family photos. *Don't land, don't land, don't land.* It spreads its wings wide, gliding down to land.

The Butterfly goes by our family photos and doesn't settle on any of the picture frames propped up on the shelf. Instead, it comes to perch on my most prized possession: silver and heart-shaped, attached to a chain of little braided metal.

My locket. The Butterfly landed on my locket.

I'm going to die.

CHAPTER THREE
The Green Blob of Past, Present, and Future

MONDAY

"YOU CAN'T DIE. YOU'RE ONLY TEN," Pepper says for what seems
like the eighth time. She puts her right hand on her chest and
hangs her head like she's in mourning. "*We're* only ten. I'm too
young to be a widowed best friend."

"I'm serious." I slam my fist on the kitchen counter, flattening a piece of yellow-orange polymer clay. Pepper's my first
and only best friend. Sometimes, though, I wonder if I should
reconsider that.

To her credit, Pepper had her dad bring her over the very next day after I saw the Butterfly. She has her faults, but I can always count on her for moral support. It didn't even matter that she lives in Antipolo, thirty minutes away from Quezon City, where I live. She still answered my call.

"So am I." Pepper raises her hands in mock surrender. They're covered with green clay slivers. *Gross.* "Stop ruining my mojo. I need it to finish this masterpiece."

I hide my snort with a cough. Pepper and I are in the kitchen, making clay sculptures. Well, at least I am. I don't want to hurt her feelings, but the mess in front of her doesn't resemble what people normally call a "masterpiece." It's more like a leafy version of the poop emoji.

"So." Pepper pokes the green glob's "head" with her pinky. "How long do you think you'll have?"

Dad said his friend had three days after the Butterfly landed on her garden spade. His cousin lasted an entire week following the insect's appearance on the tip of her fountain pen. Yet, Dad's own father didn't even make it through the first twenty-four hours. He died almost as soon as Dad saw the Butterfly sit on the space bar of my grandpa's typewriter.

"Seven days, max. Dad never told me of anyone who's lived more than that," I say, wiping sweat off my brow. The oven's already warm, but Pepper and I aren't allowed to use it on our own. Tito Ed will set our clay art into the oven to bake when he finishes his phone call. It should have been Ate Nadine. As usual, she's off doing some writerly thing.

Pepper eyes her sculpture and decides that she's done. She dumps her "artwork" onto the parchment-lined baking tray set on the counter, next to a sculpture that I made earlier. Mine is a grown-up version of a Pekin duck. White, with an orange beak and legs. It's far from being great, like Dad's creations. Still, it's better than Pepper's.

I don't want to offend my friend, but curiosity gets the better of me. "What's that supposed to be anyway?"

"It's abstract art," she says, sticking a piece of rolled black clay on top of her glob. It now looks like a green poop emoji with a decayed unicorn horn. "It's a mess, but you need to look closer. It's a beautiful representation of my past, present, and future."

I blink. "Okay."

Pepper bursts out laughing. "I'm kidding," she says, shaking her head. "I don't know what it's supposed to be either. Let's call it Algae Monster or something."

"How about the 'Green Blob of Past, Present, and Future'?" I wiggle my eyebrows.

"Sounds good." Pepper gives me a saucy wink, and we laugh louder.

"You should learn from Christopher. Sab's dad is a great sculptor," says Tito Ed, walking into the room, his brown eyes twinkling. He's wearing gym shorts, a running belt, and a light blue shirt printed with the letters "PNP," the Philippine National Police. Warm air blasts my face as he puts the tray in the oven.

"Yeah, Dad is great!" What Dad lacks in parenting he makes up for it in artistic talent. Lucky for me, I inherited some of it. When he was in the mood to teach me a new form of art, I got the hang of it easily. My favorite was (and still is) painting with oil pastels. Dad said I had the natural skills of a true artist.

We watch through the glass as the polymer clay figurines bake. I thought they'll expand, but they don't. They look very much the same way they went in the oven.

"That's true. Juice? I harvested dalandan this morning."

Tito Ed opens the fridge. Pepper and I say yes, and he pours a glassful for each of us. "Ah. That's refreshing."

It sure is. These local oranges are much sweeter than the American ones found in the grocery. Kind of like Valencia oranges, but the skin is green like a lime's—or Pepper's horrible clay art.

Pepper lets out a loud burp. "Tito Ed, what do you think about black butterflies predicting death?"

I give her a warning look, but Pepper simply shrugs.

"I try not to." Tito Ed smiles. The lines on the sides of his eyes deepen. Ate Nadine said people who smiled a lot had those "happy person" face lines. But when she realized I was talking about Tito Ed, she took it back and said they're "old people" face lines. "Why do you ask?"

"Nothing." If Pepper felt my nudge under the table, she didn't let on. "I heard Papa's staff talking about it at the farm."

It's amazing how my friend can come up with lies on the fly.

"Your mother will kill me if she finds out I've been indulging this kind of questions." Tito Ed frowns. He downs his dalandan juice in one gulp.

Tito Ed doesn't like breaking rules—especially his rules—but I know he cares about me.

I stare at him and plead with my eyes. I'm pretty sure I resemble a featherless owl who had too much coffee instead of an adorable kitten. But Pepper's doing the same thing, and she does the "cute kitty" look well.

"All right." Tito Ed sighs. "Don't tell Ginnette."

Pepper pretends to zip her lips. "Promise."

"I don't know much, but my mother used to say that black butterflies are souls of the departed." Tito Ed gathers our empty glasses and brings them to the sink. "It's the form they take when they visit loved ones."

Pepper glances at me. "Are they real?"

I take a deep breath and release the air little by little. I do this a couple of times, but my pulse isn't getting any slower.

Tito Ed takes his time before answering. He brings out the clay and turns off the oven. "It depends on you."

My friend and I exchange confused looks.

"The Butterfly's only real if you want it to be real." Tito Ed wraps the baked clay in a dry towel. "Don't touch them yet; they're still hot. You might burn your fingers."

Pepper's blue eyes narrow. They remind me of Ate Nadine's when she's annoyed. "That doesn't make any sense!"

"No, it doesn't. Don't worry yourselves about old superstitious tales, girls. It won't do you good seeing signs everywhere." Tito Ed chuckles as he fills a plastic bottle with water, securing it on his utility belt. "Ginnette thinks this belief in butterflies is just a way for grieving families to cope." He shakes his finger at us. "She's right, of course."

Pepper and I exchange a grin. It's funny how somebody as strong and tough as Tito Ed could be so scared of my small and thin mother.

Beep-beep, beep-beep!

"Time for my run." Tito Ed presses a button on his sports watch, stopping the alarm. "See you later, girls. Don't go near the oven. You might burn yourselves. I won't be long."

Mom's boyfriend leaves through the back door. When I'm sure he's outside, I bring out my inhaler and take a puff. It releases the heaviness in my chest.

Pepper tilts her head to one side, studying me. "You okay?"

"I'm fine." Physically, yes. But inside? Definitely not. "Maybe I should write a will."

I don't have anything of real value to bequeath, except for my phone and tablet. Pepper can have them. Ate Nadine might have some use for my art stuff, and Mom can donate my clothes and dolls to charity or something.

"You're not going to write a will. That's silly. Wills are for old people." Pepper takes out some fresh purple clay and starts turning it into a ball. "You heard Tito Ed. Stop worrying. Besides, you have a lot of flowers in your garden. Papa says butterflies love them."

The piece of clay I've been shaping somehow starts to resemble butterfly wings.

Nope. I'm not making a butterfly.

I slice it like cake with the plastic sculpting knife, mashing the pieces one by one.

"Our windows have screens, Pepper," I say, returning the clay back to its tray. "They keep mosquitos out, not to mention butterflies."

Pepper rolls another clay chunk into a ball. This time, a pink one. "A caterpillar could have snuck in and turned into a butterfly. It's not like you don't open the doors to get out."

It's pretty far-fetched, but it's possible. After all, we do see a lot of millipedes coming in from the garden during the rainy season. A caterpillar could have done the same. "But it was so big. Abnormally big. It freaked Lawin out too."

"Ducks get freaked out by anything—maybe an ant bit his butt. And your eyes could have been playing tricks on you. You did say the dust made them itchy, right?" Pepper leans closer, looking straight at me. I can feel my worries dissolving. "Come on. You know I'm making sense. I always make sense. I'm a genius."

"Yeah, you are." A small smile forms on my lips. Pepper might be an awful sculptor, but she *is* smart. Still, I can't shake the possibility that the Butterfly is real. Tito Ed didn't say it *wasn't*. "But I don't know . . . What if this is it?" I push my tools and ruined sculpture to the side, and lay my head on the table.

"Fine. Let's say it's true, that you *did* see the Butterfly." Pepper stops rolling the clay. I can feel her eyes on me. "You'll be dead in a week."

"Thanks a lot." I love Pepper, and her straightforwardness has always been part of her charm. But this is *my death* we're talking about. She might want to be a bit more sensitive.

"That came out wrong. I'm sorry." Pepper gets off the kitchen stool and walks over to my side. "What I'm trying to say is we shouldn't wait for your death to happen. *In case* it does happen. If we do, you're going to ruin the last days of your life moping around and feeling sorry for yourself."

I bury my face in my arms, but Pepper grabs my shoulders and pulls me upright.

"It'll be your birthday soon," she says. I struggle in Pepper's grasp, but she holds me tightly. "You're turning *eleven*, Sab. Eleven!"

"That's in a week. I'll be dead by then!" Whatever assurance Pepper gave is gone. "Dad and Ate haven't made up yet. I've never even experienced riding a jeepney. Or getting a tattoo. There are so many things I still need to do, and I'm dying already. It's not fair!"

"Hey. Calm down." Pepper lets go of me and runs her fingers through her hair. They leave tiny pieces of clay on her locks, but she doesn't seem to care. "We'll tell Ate Nadine about this Butterfly. Then she'll feel so bad she'll drive you to your papa's resort herself. If this is your last week on earth—"

"Okay, okay. I get it." I don't want to hear the possibility I might die again. Not from Pepper, not from anyone. It sounds too real. "Pepper, we can't tell Ate Nadine. Well, not yet anyway. I love your ideas—they're brilliant—but trust me on this one. We need to come up with something else before telling her about the Butterfly."

"Why?" Pepper rubs her hands on her shorts, smearing them with pink and purple clay. "You're always on my case about being honest and all that. This is just about some superstitious thing your papa said. Why is it so different?"

"It's hard to explain."

"Try me."

"It's a feeling I get." I rub the tiny piece of clay in front of me, spreading it on the table. "It's going to be harder to make her agree if we guilt her into it. She's mad at Dad about something. Like, a *huge* something. We need to fix that first."

"Not really. We need to find out what it is first." Pepper tilts her head. "Knowing your sister, we'll have more luck cracking open a diamond with a toothpick than prying that detail out of her."

My face falls. "You're right."

"Hey." Pepper grins. "Don't give up so easily."

"But you said—"

"I only said it's hard, not impossible. But first thing's first." My friend slams her fist on the clay, flattening it on the table. "I want you to promise me one thing."

"What?"

"You will stop worrying about this ridiculous Butterfly."

Maybe it's because she grew up in the United States, but Pepper would never understand why superstitions aren't *just* superstitions. When your dad believes in it, and his own mom believes in it—it's probably true.

Unfortunately, there's no time to convince Pepper. And I desperately need her help. "I can't guarantee I won't think about it at all," I say, carefully choosing my words. I may not agree with her, but Pepper *is* my best friend. I can't bring myself to lie to her. "But I'm going to try."

Pepper clasps her hands together. "That's good enough for me."

CHAPTER FOUR

Doing Butterfly Research Isn't the Same as Worrying about the Butterfly

The Black Swallowtail

(Papilio polyxenes)

The black swallowtail, also called the American swallowtail or parsnip swallowtail, is a butterfly commonly found in Oklahoma and New Jersey. Its caterpillar is called "the parsley worm" because it likes to eat parsley. The species is named after the youngest daughter of King Priam of Troy in Greek mythology, Polyxena—

* Close tab *

Are black butterflies spirits of the dead?

Question posted on 15 March 2017 at 11:46 a.m.

My brother says black butterflies are ghosts masquerading as omens. Is that true? He says I should sign my car to him just in case I die tomorrow.

* Show answer *

Are black butterflies spirits of the dead?

Answer posted on 15 March 2017 at 1:20 p.m.

Don't be ridiculous. Your brother is a selfish **CENSORED** who wants to take your car and leave you in the dust. You should disown him, or better yet, throw him off the nearest—

* Close tab *

The Myth of the Butterfly

by Manila Daily Journal

Today's column is a guest post from spiritist Jorge Mystiqua. Jorge is a respected member of the Spiritist League of the Philippines, and we are happy to have him here.

[Black butterfly animation: 80% loaded]

The black butterfly has always been shrouded with mystery. It's not a common color, and its presence is often associated with death. But one thing that isn't known is that it's also a symbol of rebirth . . . a symbol of hope.

And rightfully so.

In my many journeys all over the Philippines, I have encountered stories of black butterfly sightings. Most would see the Butterfly, and days later, find themselves mourning a loved one. It's not often I hear rebirth stories, and yet, I was fortunate to stumble upon one in the small town of Gapan, Nueva Ecija.

Perla (not her real name) told me that she lost her father to cancer the previous year. Her father (let us call him Juan), though kind and caring to Perla and her siblings, took his wife, Gina (also not her real name), for granted. They separated long before Juan found out he had stage 4 cancer.

Now, like any man near Death's door, Juan sought Gina's forgiveness. She gave it to him but kept her distance. Perla said her mother still loved Juan, but the wounds simply ran too deep.

On the night Juan passed away, Perla recalled her father murmuring about a certain ring. "Yung singsing. Ibigay mo kay Gina." He kept repeating "The ring. Give it to Gina" over and over again.

Since Perla didn't know what ring she was looking for, she simply gave her mother all her father's rings. But none of them meant anything to Gina.

On the first anniversary of Juan's death, Perla and her family celebrated Juan's babang-luksa. (For our international readers, *babang-luksa* is literally translated as "descent from mourning." It is believed that this is when the soul of the departed finally leaves earth, transitioning to that plane where spirits roam.) Perla was sitting on her late father's office desk when she saw the ominous black butterfly land on a plastic ring from a soda bottle. It stayed there for a few seconds, before flying away and out the open window.

Perla asked her mother if the plastic ring was of any importance to her father. To her surprise, Gina began to cry. Through her tears she explained the plastic ring was the one Juan presented to her when he first proposed. He was too poor to buy her a ring but swore to get her a new one. He eventually did. All along Gina thought Juan threw the plastic ring away. But he kept it, and in his last breath, wanted her to have it.

It was through the black butterfly that Juan was able to send his message across.

Are some black butterflies messengers from the dead? Could be. But I am more inclined to believe that they are the dead themselves— restless souls with unfinished business, tied to this world in the form of a black butterfly.

What then, is this black butterfly? Is it a warning, or is it a message? Is it the soul of our departed loved one, visiting us from the other side?

I cannot tell you for certain, as I have to traverse the spirit world myself to confirm.

Print

CHAPTER FIVE
Change Is Coming

TUESDAY

I PROMISED PEPPER I'M GOING to *try* not to worry about the Butterfly. But it doesn't mean I should go on with my life believing I didn't see it. Because I did. I know I did.

Besides, my research helped lessen my worries. It's possible I might not die, that maybe Dad changed his Butterfly stories a bit to make them more interesting. The last article did say the Butterfly could be a loved one's spirit or a harmless messenger from the dead.

Still, I want to make sure I get to do a few things I've always wanted to try in case I do die. Like, for example, getting my hair dyed blue.

Honestly, I'm surprised Ate Nadine agreed to take me to the salon. It's not far from where we live, and it's right across from her college, but it's still a fifteen-minute drive away from home. Fifteen minutes without traffic, that is.

I'm leaning back comfortably on the styling chair when Pepper drops the bomb.

"Sab says she's going to die."

I gasp. "Pepper!"

"What? Ate Nadine needs to know." My friend looks at me with innocent eyes. I glare at her. We both know that's not why she wanted to tell Ate Nadine. Pepper swipes at her phone screen, and the wobbly robot walks to the edge of a grassy cliff. It survives the fall to the water, but it's now walking back and forth aimlessly, unable to climb back up the puzzle tower. There's a squeaking sound as Pepper slams her hand on the armrest of her styling chair. "Ugh! I've been stuck on this level for two days."

We had been peacefully waiting for the salon staff to attend to us. That is, until Pepper decided to ruin the moment.

"Is that so?" Ate Nadine asks from my right, where she's lounging on a styling chair with a magazine.

"Maybe Ate Nadine can do something about it." Sighing, Pepper saves her game and slips the phone into her shorts pocket. "Or maybe talk some sense into you."

"I saw the Butterfly, Ate," I explain, pausing to rub my nostrils. The strong scents of nail polish and hair spray are giving me a headache. "The one Dad—"

"I remember Dad's butterfly stories," Nadine says. "But Dad has said a lot of things, and not all of them are true. In fact, it's thanks to his lies that I'm going to be a journalist."

I don't believe her. Dad didn't lie to us. He couldn't have lied to her so badly that it merited a yearlong cold shoulder and her choice to pick a degree specializing in searching for truths. Anyway, Ate Nadine has always wanted to be a writer since forever.

Ate Nadine puts down her magazine and studies me. "Does getting this new hairdo have anything to do with that butterfly?"

She never misses anything. No wonder a top newspaper wanted Ate Nadine as an intern.

"Yes. Definitely," Pepper chirps. She leans back on the styling chair and closes her eyes. "If Sab's going to die like the Butterfly predicted, she might as well have a little fun with her hair."

"You're lucky I have something I need to do in this neighborhood later. Or I wouldn't have bothered with this nonsense." My sister turns her attention to the television screen hanging from the corner of the ceiling. "Now be quiet and leave me in peace."

My face falls. I was hoping my sister would tell me *something*. Tito Ed's explanation was cryptic and uncertain. The most I got from my internet search was an editorial from the newspaper Ate Nadine is interning for. I was hoping my sister could tell me what she knows of the Butterfly. And yet, she's acting like it's not real—just because it was Dad who told her about it.

But then again, if Ate Nadine says the Butterfly's not real, she's probably right. I'm just worrying myself over nothing.

The stylist rolls a cart full of dyeing solutions between Ate Nadine and me. I totally forget about the Butterfly.

I've always wanted mermaid hair. To curl my limp hair

and dye its locks with varying shades of turquoise, purple, and aqua blue. But I knew Mom would forbid it, just as she did with Ate Nadine.

Dad told me Ate wanted to have unicorn-pink hair when she was twelve. Mom was totally against it. Since she's as stubborn as my sister, Dad couldn't change her mind. So, he bought Ate Nadine this expensive set of pink hair chalk. It allowed my sister to get pink hair whenever she wanted and rinse it off before Mom could see.

I didn't think Ate Nadine would agree so easily to me getting my hair dyed. But I guess she did remember what it felt like to want something and be forbidden to get it. Or maybe—*just maybe*—she remembered what Dad did for her.

I'm hoping it's the latter.

"Can you turn the volume up, please?" my sister asks the lady doing her manicure. "I didn't get to watch the news last night."

Of course Ate Nadine didn't have time to watch the news. She barricaded herself in her room, working on that assignment of hers. Tito Ed had to knock on her door himself to get Ate Nadine to eat dinner.

I'm seriously starting to hate that assignment. It's taking way too much of my sister's time. I could die right here at the salon and she'd probably still be worrying about it instead of me.

The newly elected president of the Philippines appears on TV. The reporter says he's at a conference giving a speech. I'd love to tell you more about what he's saying, but I can't. Loud bleeps censor almost every word he utters.

"I love that man." The stylist chuckles as he helps me put on a hairdressing cape. The smooth fabric cascades from my shoulders all the way to the floor.

I raise my eyebrows. "He says a lot of bad words."

"Yeah." From the mirror, I see Pepper nod in agreement. "Papa curses a lot too, but the president is, like, twenty times worse."

"It's just the way he is." The stylist laughs again. He tucks his bright green hair behind his ears, then works the lever that shifts my chair into reclining position. He doesn't stop until I'm almost lying down. "He's a good president, and he'll deliver his campaign promise—'Change is coming.' He'll save the Philippines with what he's doing."

The manicurist lowers the volume as commercials replace the news feature. Ate Nadine thanks the woman and twists around in her chair to meet my stylist's gaze. "People are dying because of him."

"If you're not doing or selling drugs, there's nothing for you to be afraid of," the stylist says. I can't see what he's doing, but I hear him roll another cart behind me. "The war on drugs isn't just about the police operations, darling. My brother-in-law is a drug addict, but he's trying to do better with help from his local government. Their rehab program is part of the war on drugs campaign."

"That's true," Ate Nadine admits. "But you heard him. The president's threatened to kill all those involved in the drug trade. That includes your own brother-in-law."

"I don't think he means that. The president knows what he's doing." The stylist puts a rolled towel under my neck, then gathers my hair. I almost jump when he sprays my head with cold water. "Sorry, darling, but I need to wash your hair."

"He should condemn the killings, not encourage them," Ate Nadine says as the stylist lathers shampoo on me. The fragrance overpowers the icky smell of nail polish with ylang-ylang blossoms and grapefruit. "There are people who will take everything he says literally. Words have power, you know."

Pepper lets out a loud yawn beside me, and I can't help but

imitate her. The shampoo has a relaxing effect. I shift to a more comfortable position on the recliner, tuning out Ate Nadine's boring political commentary.

I love the smell of ylang-ylang. It reminds me of Lola Cordia's perfume and her resort in Pililla. We used to go there regularly when she was still alive. We often caught the ylang-ylang trees surrounding the butterfly garden in full bloom, usually in the summer. Now would be the perfect time to go there, if only my sister wanted to.

"Ate Nadine is a journalist," I say with pride. Writing keeps her away from me most times, but not many college freshmen can say they're working for a national paper. "She's an intern for the *Manila Daily Journal*."

The stylist gently turns my head back to its original position and begins washing the suds off my locks. From the mirror I see him meet my sister's gaze. "Don't waste your talent on that paper, darling. They're fake news who like to sensationalize events to make the president look bad."

"They are not."

Uh-oh. I smell trouble.

"Oh? Then why is that paper insisting the fire at the mall is a terrorist attack?" The stylist brings my chair back to the sitting position and proceeds to dry my hair. "The police were able to prove an angry employee started it."

Ate Nadine scowls. I can almost see the counterarguments she's thinking, popping over her head like thought bubbles in a comic book. It makes me worried for my hair.

"*Okay,*" Pepper chimes in from beside me. She squeezes her head. "I think we're done with all the boring stuff. My brain is exploding."

"Mine too." I imitate her, then take a lock of my blow-dried hair. "If I also add some pink, will it be too much?"

Ate Nadine rolls her eyes. Through the mirror, I can see her expression soften. "You two are hopeless."

The stylist chuckles and proceeds to open a bottle of solution. "We'll see. But first we need to bleach your hair. The colors won't be visible if it's all black like that."

It's amazing how Pepper manages to diffuse a situation. One day, I've got to learn to do just that. Pepper won't always be around to save me from getting a bad haircut.

"Wait." Ate Nadine stops the stylist. "Sab's never had her hair treated. She could be allergic."

The stylist obliges and applies a drop of solution on my wrist. It doesn't take a minute for my skin to turn red. He does the same for the hair dye, and the reaction is the same: I'm allergic.

"I'm sorry," says the stylist, his eyes full of pity. He pats his short green locks. "How about a new hairstyle? Having pretty hair isn't just about color."

I turn to my left, where the attendant is done with Ate Nadine's fingernails and is now readying her for a pedicure.

My sister dips her feet in solution. "If you really want something different, you can let him cut your hair."

"A trim?"

Ate Nadine shakes her head, smiling. "No. Whatever you want."

"Oh!" Pepper grabs the hairstyle catalog from the table in front of her. "I'll help you pick one."

"What about Mom?" I glance at the styles Pepper is considering. "She'll be furious."

"I'll talk to her," Ate Nadine says with a wink. "Well?"

I see everyone staring at me, eagerly awaiting my decision.

I've always kept my hair long. Mom said I should wait until I actually have boobs so no one mistakes me for a boy if I cut it short.

But Mom's not here. I can do what I want. If I'm still alive by the time she gets back, she'll definitely get mad at me. But if I'm dead like the Butterfly foretold . . . well, I might as well leave this world in style.

Like the president said, "Change is coming." I take a deep breath and exhale aloud. "Let's do it."

CHAPTER SIX
Children of the Dew

IT'S ONLY HALF PAST THREE when Pepper and I step out of the salon and onto the strip mall lanai. The sun's still up, but its heat isn't as searing as it was at lunchtime.

I touch my hair. The stylist shaved the area right above my nape. Whenever I run my hand over it, I feel like I'm stroking a short-haired cat. It feels so weird.

During the school year, Mom and Tito Ed drove me by this strip mall every day on my way to school. I'd stick my face to the glass, wishing to stroll down its walkways, which are lined with palm trees and blue flower bushes. Or maybe roam the open-sided gallery on its second floor. Ate Nadine always talked about hanging out with her friends there. But it's always crowded, and finding a parking space is next to impossible, so we opt for the bigger malls along Marcos Highway instead.

Ate Nadine, on the other hand, knows where to leave the car even when the strip mall's parking is full. Her school, San Jose Pignatelli College, is right across the street. Today there are still a lot of people, but less than usual, since it's summer.

"You shouldn't have told Ate Nadine." I'm not mad at Pepper, but I'm not letting her off the hook that easily. "It could have gone down very badly, you know."

"It didn't, and now we can at least say we tried. Back to the original plan then. Figure out what happened to your papa and sister, fix it, and we can all go to the resort together." Pepper leans over the balustrade. "Besides, you promised not to worry about the Butterfly thing, then I saw that article on your desk. I knew you couldn't resist it. You broke your promise, so it's only fair that I can break mine."

"I didn't technically break it, you know. I only said I'd try. And I did *try*," I say, joining her.

"Fair enough." Pepper gives me a nudge. "But you know I'm right. Aren't you feeling a bit better now? I mean, you were such a mess yesterday. Even worse than my clay masterpiece!"

I nudge her back. "Nothing's worse than that awful thing."

We laugh, eventually lapsing to a cozy silence.

This strip mall is one of newer buildings in the area, quite like Ate Nadine's school. An open-air pedestrian walkway connects the two establishments, overlooking public jeepneys and private cars traveling in moderate traffic.

Garish decorations and graffiti-like paintings adorn the jeepneys. They provide a stark contrast to the college's modern buildings, color-coordinated flower gardens, and manicured, tree-lined lawns.

Like Ate Nadine, Mom and Dad went to San Jose Pignatelli College as well. It was also the place where they first met. Pepper and I had talked about studying there together one day. She'll take up a business course, while I'll pick the one that suits me most—something related to the arts.

"Psst!"

There's no one else on the strip mall lanai but my friend and me. Pepper continues to watch the clouds as though she can't hear anything.

"PSST!"

Against my better judgment, I look down to the parking area below. Instead of passengers waiting for the next jeepney to stop, a group of boys my age are hanging out under a waiting shed. Their shirts and shorts are dirty and tattered, making my after-art-session clothes seem neat and clean. Most of them carry white garlands of sampaguita flowers. The others, a tower of pot holders or pirated DVDs.

A boy, who looks just a few years older than Pepper and me, meets my gaze. There's a huge scar running down his right cheek, like somebody tried to slash his face. The boy points at me, then at Pepper, puckering his lips.

"Gross!"

The other kids laugh aloud and give each other high fives.

"Ugh." I turn around to face the salon, leaning my back on the balustrade. Pepper does the same. "I thought Tito Ed said that the president ordered the police to get the batang hamog off the streets."

Batang hamog is a directly translated as "children of the dew." It sounds poetic, and very appropriate to describe children who live on the streets exposed to evening dewdrops. But Ate Nadine said the term *batang hamog* is now unfortunately associated with streets kids causing mischief and committing crimes.

Over a year ago, there was news about a gang of batang

hamog high on drugs terrorizing drivers in the middle of traffic. If caught, the batang hamog and their parents would threaten the cops with child-abuse lawsuits. The police would then have to let the bad kids go.

Well, that is until the new president came to office. No wonder there are a lot of adults like my stylist who idolize him.

"They're not batang hamog. Just jerks," Pepper says, shaking her head. "Papa used to bring me in with him to his missionary work at a rehab center. There were often new kids who came in—most of them batang hamog—when they were still high. You could see it in their eyes—they all had this scary look in them. Like they're dead inside."

I reach over to take Pepper's hand and give it a squeeze. We look through the clear glass windows of the salon, where there's a commotion behind the cashier. Ate Nadine's frown has turned to a scowl as she continues to wait in line.

"They better let Ate Nadine pay before she explodes," Pepper says with a wry smile. She lifts the front of her shirt. "It's so humid, and I'm icky. Wish I had your hair."

"I feel like I've gone bald," I say, touching the shaved area above my neck. I try to tuck hair behind my ear, but the short locks just fall back to my forehead. "Tell me again why I ever thought a pixie cut was a good idea."

"It's gorgeous! Stop touching it." Pepper takes my wrist and gives it a playful slap. "I would have gotten a Mohawk if I didn't promise my cousin I won't have any makeovers until after her wedding this coming Saturday."

"Really?" If I were her cousin, I wouldn't want a junior bridesmaid with a Mohawk either.

"Why not? It'll grow back. Besides, it's summer. My hair gets sweaty at night even with the AC—I mean, *aircon*—on full blast." Pepper wipes the sweat off her brow. "We've been friends for three years already, and I've never seen you do something this different till now."

"I know." When a supernatural insect warns you of possible death, you can't help but be a little bit braver and actually do things you've always wanted to do.

The chimes above the salon door tinkle, and we see Ate Nadine emerge.

"It's still early," she says, checking the time on her phone. "Who wants ice cream?"

Pepper raises her hand. "Me!"

As I'm about to agree, my eyes wander down to where the rude boys are. They aren't there anymore, except for one.

Like the others, his green shirt and red basketball shorts are worn and full of holes, hanging on his thin frame like a scarecrow. He's much older than the rude boys, probably as old as Ate Nadine. He has thick eyebrows, dark brown skin, and a high-bridged nose. His black hair is longer than my newly short cut. He doesn't look like he's selling anything, sitting on the bench as though he's waiting for something. Or someone.

There's something off about this guy, and he's staring at us.

Could he be one of those kids who managed to escape the president's purge? Lola Cordia had warned my father about them. I overheard her tell Dad about a TV news report on a group of batang hamog so out of it they stabbed and killed a child.

My heart rate jumps to asthma-episode levels. I exhale slowly, trying to control my breathing.

Is this guy the one to seal my fate? Is he the one the Butterfly warned me about?

I hadn't thought about *how* I'd go, but now I wonder if this is it. He doesn't have big muscles or anything, but he's not sickly thin either. I'm pretty sure he's strong enough to harm me if he wanted to.

"Sab." I feel a hand on my back. It's Pepper's. "Ice cream?"

"Ah. Yes. Sorry." I tear my gaze away from the boy. "Of course I want ice cream."

"What were you looking at?" Ate Nadine walks to the railing and looks down. "There's nothing there."

I blink. My sister's right. The boy's gone.

"There's no point trying to make sense of something that makes no sense in the first place." With a sigh, Ate Nadine takes me by the shoulders. "You really need to stop worrying about this Butterfly. I'm here. I promise I won't let anything bad happen to you."

My breathing slows. I'm wary of promises, but something tells me she'll keep this one. Ate Nadine has always taken care of me ever since Dad left and Mom started going on business trips. Tito Ed's around, but it's Ate Nadine I depend on.

I twist the chain of my locket around my index finger. "Does the ice cream place have cheese flavor?"

"Of course." Ate Nadine smiles. It's reassuring and calming somehow. Like it can lift the weight of the world off my shoulders. And it does.

For the time being.

CHAPTER SEVEN
The Alley of Knickknacks and Skin Whiteners

THE STRIP MALL HAS RESTAURANTS with unique specialties. It also has a shop selling sporting goods and a bookstore where college students hang out. I want to go in and replenish my art tools, but I don't mind waiting until we've eaten. We pass by a café, where my sister greets classmates smoking cigarettes and sipping lattes. My mouth waters at the smell of steaming hot cocoa and freshly baked donuts coming from a pastry shop, but Ate Nadine keeps on walking.

Pepper's face falls. "Oh, I thought we were having dessert."

"We are." Ate Nadine takes our hands as we cross a

narrow side street, navigating parked cars and vendors. "Stay close to me."

I don't argue, nor does Pepper. We all know I'm the worst when it comes to crossing a street. I doubt cars here would stop for me the way they do in our neighborhood. We aren't far from home, but it's not a place where Mom would usually allow Pepper and me to roam. I don't blame her.

When I was four and Ate Nadine was the same age as I am now, Dad brought us along to a place much like this alley. Full of people, parked cars, and goods for sale. Maybe it was because Dad left us with his friend at the bakery while he went to his meeting, but alleys like this are just way too scary for me. They're chaotic and wild, so unlike our peaceful gated subdivision.

My sister doesn't let go even after we've turned right into an alley between two low-rise apartments. One is stark white, with a simple, modern design. The other seems like it hasn't seen the cleaners since the day Ate Nadine was born. I feel like I'll get hives just by looking at its algae-covered walls.

Vendors litter the sides of the buildings. They sell stuff from cell phone accessories to pirated DVDs. Unbranded beauty products, cheap gadgets, and knickknacks are spread out on wooden trays. Rubber phone and tablet covers hang on display racks.

There's a food cart halfway down the alleyway, but it's still too far to see what they're selling. There's smoke snaking up from the cart. I doubt that's where we're going.

My tummy grumbles. "Where's the ice cream?"

"We're near. It's right there at the corner." Ate Nadine lets go of our hands and points to a corner shop at the end of the alley. "Are you tired? Do you want to rest—"

"Miss! Come and take a look." A scrawny woman approaches my sister, waving a plastic bottle at her face. "For thirty pesos, you can become as beautiful as this white girl. Generic only, but it's better than the skin whiteners you buy at the grocery. Here, try some!"

"Get away from me," Ate Nadine growls. "It's because of people like you that we Filipinos can't ever get past this awful colonial mentality. Just because someone's white doesn't mean they're prettier or better."

I feel the need to hide whenever my sister gives me that look. But the woman vendor simply shrugs and proceeds to hound other passersby.

"I keep telling her the insults will not get customers," says another vendor, a man with graying hair. He gives us a warm smile. Upon closer look, he's got a couple of teeth missing. "I believe your brown skin makes you even prettier. You do not need whitening lotion."

"Salamat po, Mang Larry," Ate Nadine thanks the vendor, referring to him as Mr. Larry. My sister seems to know a lot of people here. She gives the man a smile. "You leave me no choice but to buy from you."

Mang Larry laughs. "Be my guest."

"Are those stickers?" Pepper asks as she looks over my shoulder. Her breath is warm on my ear.

"Some." Mang Larry nods. He waves his hand around the left half of the merchandise. "These are temporary tattoos."

If not for the label in almost-unintelligible scrawl, it's hard to distinguish the stickers from the tattoos. They come in all different colors and designs—cartoon characters, dragons, flowers, and cute animals. There's even a llama sticker *and* temporary tattoo. Why anyone would want a llama on their skin, I have no idea.

"Ohh! Can we get some, Ate Nadine?" Pepper exclaims. She points to a tattoo between an angry lion and a cute cat. "Look, Sab! It's perfect for you."

It's an image of a butterfly. It has wings of intricate swirls and florals. Definitely not *the* Butterfly. Still—

"Nope." I don't need a constant reminder that I'm going to die. "Not that one."

"Aw, come on." Pepper rolls her eyes. It's the same look Ate Nadine gives me whenever I say something she finds ridiculous. "You need to face your fears. I mean, if you really are going to die—"

I give my friend a pointed look. Sure, she finds the idea of the Butterfly silly. I can't stop her from feeling that way, but I wish she'd talk about my impending doom with a little more care.

"Sab's not going to die." Ate Nadine snorts. She picks up the butterfly tattoo. "You're not afraid of butterflies—you're scared of dying. Not all butterflies bring death."

I study the tattoo in Ate Nadine's hand. It's so much smaller than Dad's Butterfly, and its colors are mint green and purple, my favorites.

Ate Nadine's right. This butterfly tattoo won't bring me death. It's just a tattoo, and a temporary one at that.

"Okay, I'll get that one." I point to the tattoo, as if daring it to come and take me.

"Awesome!" Pepper lets out a loud whoop. "Lemme pick mine."

"Ate, do you remember that tattoo parlor in Libis, the one where Dad used to get inked?" I ask, holding out the back of my hand as my sister dips the butterfly stick-on tattoo in Mang Larry's cup of water. "I wonder if it's still open."

"I don't know and I don't care. Hold still," my sister orders. She rubs the wet tattoo facedown on my skin. It's surprisingly cold, considering the hot afternoon weather. "And don't even bother. Mom's never going to let you get anything permanent."

As if I'd have the courage to get one. Like Mom, needles terrify me. The very thought of a pointy object poking my skin repeatedly makes me want to faint. "Mom never liked Daddy getting inked, did she?"

"With good reason." Ate Nadine peels it off like a sticker, leaving behind the butterfly image on my hand. "Those tattoos are expensive."

A frown etches across my face. I feel like I missed something. "So why did you keep accompanying him?"

"So he wouldn't spend all our money on those pesky tattoos." Ate Nadine's eyes narrow dangerously. She avoids my gaze, looking over my shoulder. "Somebody had to be an adult when he obviously didn't want to."

I take a deep breath, exhaling slowly. That's not how I remember it. Dad cares about us. He would never have spent money if it meant making it difficult for our family. Ate Nadine's wrong. "But Dad didn't—"

"Enough, Sab."

"Hey." Pepper puts down the llama tattoo. "Sab's just asking questions. You don't have to—"

"I said, enough!"

I wince at Ate Nadine's tone and take a step back. Pepper, on the other hand, simply shrugs. She wets her llama tattoo in Mang Larry's water cup and proceeds to apply the design on her left arm. How she's able to remain unaffected by Ate's temper, I have no idea.

"You keep putting Dad on a pedestal, like he can do no wrong." Ate Nadine pays for my tattoo and Pepper's. She doesn't even bother counting her change. Her nostrils are flaring, her eyes blazing. "Don't make the same mistake I did, Sab. There are things about him . . . You have no idea—ugh!"

The fury leaves my sister's eyes, like flipping a switch. Her frown remains, but it looks worried now instead of angry.

She's looking off down the street. "Stay here. I won't be long. Mang Larry, my sister . . . could you—"

"I'll look after them." The vendor nods. "They're safe with me. Do what you need to do for that article of yours."

"Ate, what's wrong?" But my sister doesn't seem to hear. She hurries into the crowd of shoppers and disappears.

"Let her go." Pepper pats my shoulder. "She's just upset."

"It's not that." It's hard to keep my voice even. My breath comes out in between gasps. I reach behind me, trying to get the inhaler without removing my backpack. Ate Nadine said while we were at the salon that Dad's lies became the reason why she took up journalism. I didn't really believe her. But now? I don't know. "What do you think Ate meant? She said something about Dad doing bad things."

"You look weird, all twisty like that. Here." Pepper gets the medicine from my bag, handing it to me. I take a puff and let her continue. "Ate Nadine said 'things about him.' She didn't say they were bad. You're worrying yourself for nothing again."

It's my turn to frown. "It's usually bad when people do things that make you not talk to them for a year."

"That's true." Pepper tilts her head to one side, the way she does when she's thinking. She counts her fingers. "We only have six days left before your birthday. If we're to figure out why your sister hates your papa, we need to hurry. Because, from the looks of it, their issues might be bigger than we initially thought."

Actually, *I* knew the issues between my sister and dad were serious. Pepper was the only one who thought otherwise.

We hang out near Mang Larry's cart for only a moment more, and then Pepper's blue eyes light up like a bulb. "Let's follow Ate Nadine," she says. "See what she's up to."

"Not sure that's a good idea." I want to know what Ate Nadine's doing, but I'm not sure if I *need* to know. She's probably doing some writerly thing, which I doubt has any relevance to her issues with Dad. It's not worth risking her temper again, especially when she's already mad at me. Ate Nadine is very particular about everyone respecting her privacy. Spying on her sounds like the opposite of that. Pepper is just being nosy.

"Here I am thinking you're fun now," Pepper says, rolling her eyes. "Your sister won't see us. Papa bought a DVD collection of the entire five seasons of *Chuck*. I've been learning a lot about spying and stuff! There's this episode where the CIA agent won't tell Chuck about a case—"

Before I can tell Pepper I don't really care about Chuck's

adventures, I see someone familiar across the alley. He looks at me, and I at him.

Green shirt, red shorts. Age eighteen or nineteen. Haunting eyes framed by pretty lashes.

He's the same guy I saw under the waiting shed. The one who seemingly disappeared.

"Sab?"

I blink. "Can you see that man?"

"The one with the baggy clothes?" Pepper says as she looks over my shoulder. "Yeah. Why?"

I didn't imagine him. The thought makes my stomach turn. "I think he's out to get us."

CHAPTER EIGHT
The Great Kwek-Kwek Duo

WHEN I TOLD PEPPER ABOUT the creepy guy, I knew she wouldn't take me seriously. She thinks I worry too much about things I shouldn't worry about.

But I didn't expect her to *laugh*.

"Don't be a snob, Sab," Pepper says when she's done laughing at my expense. "Just because he doesn't dress like you doesn't mean he's dangerous."

I grit my teeth. Pepper doesn't get it.

The man is leaning on the wall of the dingy apartment building, just a few vendors away from the rude lady who tried to sell Ate Nadine skin whiteners. He keeps looking from left to right, but his gaze always lingers when it passes by our general direction. It's too suspicious to ignore.

"He's been lurking around, Pepper," I insist. "He was there at the waiting shed, staring at us, and now he's followed us here."

It's hard to explain, but it's a gut feeling I have. He's bad news. I don't care if Pepper doesn't believe in the Butterfly. I'm not going to risk it. I just know this man is following us.

"Calm down. Geez." Pepper rolls her eyes in a very Ate-Nadine-like fashion. You know, the eye roll that never fails to make me feel ridiculous. "He won't hurt anyone."

"But Ate—"

"Fine. Let's move closer to your sister without her knowing. If that man still follows us, then you're right. Now stay behind me." Pepper pushes me aside, and I do as she ordered. My friend puts on a big smile and walks up to the tattoo vendor. She points at the food cart down the alley. "Mang Larry, we're really hungry. We were supposed to eat with Ate Nadine, but she left. Can we buy food from there?"

Mang Larry purses his lips, and Pepper's innocent blue eyes turn big and round. I can see his defenses melting already. No one can resist Pepper's charms.

I rub my tummy for effect. The big-eyed look never works for me. I'm just not white and pretty enough.

"Very well," Mang Larry says with a sigh. "Don't go far, children. This alley might be generally safe, but there are bad folks lurking about."

There's only one bad person lurking about, and it's that man.

The food-cart attendant is frying hard-boiled quail eggs covered in orange tempura-like batter. The stench of gas from the portable stove is far from appetizing. Still, the sizzling sound of kwek-kwek as they float in the oil is music to my ears—and stomach.

"Six pieces for me, please," Pepper says as she fishes coins from her purse. The vendor drops kwek-kwek in a plastic cup for Pepper. "Sab, you better tell him how many you want, because I'm going to finish all these."

"Are you serious?" I ignore the vendor and glare at my friend. "You said we're following Ate Nadine! Now we've lost her."

Pepper squeezes spiced vinegar over the fried quail eggs and uses a barbecue stick to stuff one inside her mouth. *"Can-spa-we-uhm-huh-gri."*

"What?" I take a step back as kwek-kwek bits land on my arm. "Gross!"

With a totally unapologetic grin, Pepper swallows, wiping her mouth on the back of her hand. "I said, I can't spy when I'm hungry. Chuck says in season one that you should always have food when you're on a stakeout. The man's gone, by the way. He would have followed us if he had bad intentions. As for your sister . . ." Before I can protest, she points across the alley. "Look over there."

The scrawny vendor lady sits on a stool beside her huge tray of skin whiteners. People (particularly women) scowl as they pass her by, probably because she's using insults to sell her products. Behind her is a revolving stand full of colorful cell phone cases, where a young woman is browsing—Ate Nadine.

I frown. "She has a gazillion cases already. What does she need a new one for?"

It's unfair for Ate Nadine to get mad at Dad for spending on tattoos when she's buying every plastic case that fits her phone. Dad likes collecting tattoos. She likes collecting cases. They're both the same.

"That's not what I meant." Pepper dismisses my concern with a wave.

I squint, studying my sister closer. She's shifting through the cell phone cases, but her eyes are elsewhere and her phone is in her hand. I follow her gaze, and Pepper does the same.

A few vendors down, there are guys as old as Ate Nadine hanging out beside the apartment building's back door. A short man wearing a cap as orange as a kwek-kwek appears.

Ate Nadine lifts up her phone.

"She's spying on them." Pepper's breath reeks of spiced vinegar. "They're probably the people her boss wants her to investigate."

"I don't— Oh no!" I gasp. The guy has reappeared. This time, he's heading for Ate Nadine.

"What?"

"It's the man again. He *did* follow us!"

Pepper narrows her eyes, then they gloss over like they do when she's deep in thought. "You know, you might be right about him. But I can't be sure."

I *am* sure. I knew that man had bad intentions from the start. He's probably the leader of those batang hamog. I wouldn't be surprised if he's also a drug addict. But the thing is, he's going to hurt Ate Nadine, and I can't let that happen.

"We should wait and see. I mean, there are a lot of people in this alley. He can't just go around hurting people, especially since your sister seems to know a lot of people here . . ."

Pepper's rambling, but I'm not really hearing her anymore.

I have to do something.

Anything.

". . . I mean, those guys she's filming can't be that danger- ous, right? It's too early for them to do anything iffy. Maybe we should go back to the stickers stand. Hmm . . . Yes, that's what we should do— Sab! Where are you going?"

I hear Pepper's protests, but I ignore her. I dash across the alley, pushing my way between people and merchandise.

"Hoy!" an angry male voice calls. I ignore him too.

"Ate!" I need to get to my sister. I need to warn her. *"Ahh-teh!"*

My sister looks up from her phone, surprised. She slips the phone inside her pocket. "Sab, where's Pepper? What are you—"

A stabbing pain pierces my upper thigh as I bump into the corner of a merchandise tray. "OW!"

Bottles of skin whiteners go crashing to the ground. The scrawny woman vendor belts out a slew of curses as bad as the president's on TV—but without the bleeps.

I feel bad not helping the woman pick up her stuff, but I can't stop now. I'll say sorry later. The batang hamog leader is right behind Ate Nadine now.

"Ate, watch out!" I point at the bad guy, gasping for breath. "Behind you!"

"Sab, don't." It's Pepper. She's caught up with me, breathing as heavily as I am.

The man takes another step closer.

"Go away!" I shout. "Don't hurt her!"

"What are you talking about?" Ate Nadine spins looks around and finally sees the man. "Oh."

Oh? What does that mean, "Oh"?

I'm starting to be aware that people are gathering around us. The lotion vendor is still screaming bad words. I push the self-conscious feelings aside, but somehow, words fail me. I glance at Pepper, pleading for help.

My friend looks the man straight in the eye as she rummages through her pockets. "Is it money you want? We don't have a lot, but will this do—"

Ate Nadine bursts out laughing. "No way."

Pepper and I exchange bewildered looks.

"What's so funny with what I said?" Pepper asks, a frown spreading across her face.

To my surprise, Ate Nadine walks to the man's side. He's not laughing like her, but it's almost as if he's trying not to.

"Sorry about that," Ate Nadine tells him, patting his shoulder. "Girls, meet my friend Jepoy. I asked him to meet us here. Jepoy, the white girl is Pepper. And this judgmental one is my baby sister, Sab."

The man called Jepoy grins. His long lashes are prettier up close. "Hey."

Pepper turns red like an overripe tomato. I want to sink into the ground. Or maybe hide under the skin whiteners strewn all over the alley.

"Are you all just going to stand there?" The scrawny vendor woman has stopped cursing and screaming. She stands before us, hands on her hips, her eyes smoldering like a volcano ready to erupt. "Help me get my lotions back, you little brats!"

CHAPTER NINE
Runaway Duck

WEDNESDAY

"ATE, PHONE CALL FOR YOU." My sister's bedroom door is ajar, but I still knock. The last time I barged in uninvited, her fury nearly blasted me to smithereens.

"Come in." Ate Nadine is on the floor, right in the middle of scattered photos, opened folders, and piles of paper. "Sab, stop wasting printer ink on those useless butterfly articles. It's really annoying having it run out just when I need to print my article—"

"Phone call," I repeat. Honestly, I'm not in the mood for a lecture right now. I've had enough of getting screamed at yesterday. The angry lady vendor wouldn't stop shouting until we left the alley. I don't think I can ever look at a bottle of skin whitener the same way again. "It's your boss from the paper. She said she's been trying to reach you, but your cell phone is turned off."

Ate Nadine bounces from the floor like a jack-in-the-box, rushing past me to answer the phone downstairs. She leaves her door open and notes flying about.

I hold back the urge to roll my eyes. If my sister paid me a teeniest bit of the attention she gives her boss, I'd welcome the Butterfly's warning and die happy.

Sighing, I take Ate Nadine's cell phone and plug it in to a charger. The battery is totally empty, and she had no idea, even though it's right beside her laptop. My sister will hate me for saying this, but really, she's a lot like Dad in so many ways. They can be so focused on their work that the world around them simply disappears.

"Duck alert! Duck alert!" Pepper calls from outside Ate Nadine's room. The noisy flip-flopping of rubber slippers follows Lawin's quacking. I stick my head out into the hallway, where Pepper is running toward me. "Watch out, Sab. The door—"

Too late.

Lawin has already snuck inside, waddling straight to my sister's pile of papers on the floor. He picks up an important-looking document with his beak.

"Leave that alone, you little monster!" Pepper lunges for Lawin, but he zips past her. "Argh! Sab, get him before he—"

I try to grab the duck, but he wiggles away from me.

"—poops." Pepper groans. "We are so dead."

Forget the Butterfly. Ate Nadine is going to *kill* me.

"I'll get some wet tissue. Don't let him poop again." My friend hurries to Ate Nadine's bathroom.

Lawin struggles in my grasp, but I hold him tight under my right arm this time. "We are going to be in so much trouble." The duck lets out a raspy quack as I rummage through the wastebasket with my free hand. I take a crumpled piece of paper and use it to remove most of the poop. Thankfully, the poop didn't seep through to the stuff inside the folder. "Yeah, this is your fault. Why can't you behave for once? I let you poop in my room, but you can't do that in Ate's— Hey, I know this place!"

Inside Ate Nadine's folder labeled "For Interview" is a brochure of a facility featuring a purple-and-pink building on the main flap. I open it up and see that Ate Nadine has circled the photo of an old man in doctor's clothes.

I remember him. He had less gray hair when I saw him, but I will never forget his face. He has this perpetual scowl and two huge front teeth that make him look like a grouchy old rabbit. Maybe I just don't like him because he was the doctor who coldly told us we weren't allowed to take Daddy home.

Mom said the doctor was helping Dad with his medical condition. Well, Dad was depressed. Why would Ate Nadine want to talk to a doctor who treats depression for her article?

"I'd leave that alone, if I were you." Pepper joins me and Lawin on the floor. She dabs the wet tissue on Ate Nadine's "For Interview" folder. "You know how your sister gets when people go through her things. She'll eat you alive."

I toss her the facility flyer. "Dad went there to get treatment for his depression. Ate is going to interview his old doctor. Why?"

Pepper sighs and brings out her cell phone. There's a series of clicks as she snaps photos of the papers and folders scattered about. "There. You can stare at them later for as long as you want. Now help me clean up—"

"What are you two doing in here?" I get a sick feeling in my stomach as Ate Nadine stands before us, hands on her hips. Her eyes widen when they see the wet stain on the folder. "Oh my g— Is that poop on my notes? SAB!"

Lawin quacks in panic. His claws scratch my skin as he thrashes in my arms. From the corner of my eye, I see Pepper slide the brochure back inside the folder.

Thankfully, Ate Nadine is too furious to notice. "How many times do I have to tell you? You can't keep the duck inside the house. Ang tigas ng ulo mo."

"I'm not hardheaded!" I hug Lawin closer as I stand. He's my duck, and I can't let my sister take him away from me. "He'll be lonely out there, Ate. This won't happen again, promise. I'll potty train him."

"Hey, hey. Stop it. Keep scaring Lawin, and he'll poop again." Pepper wedges herself between my sister and me, holding her arm wide to keep us apart. "You're both right. Our ducks are happier in our yard with the pond and all. Lawin grew up with humans, so he'll get very lonely out there. And Mama said he can't be potty trained ever because he doesn't have the butt muscles to hold his poop. But there's a way."

"If you can put a giant cork into that butt, you can keep him inside." Ate Nadine crosses her arms over her chest. "If not, Mom's gonna hear about this, and that poop machine will stay in the yard."

"I don't need a cork." Pepper shakes her head. "Can I borrow your sewing kit?"

"It's in the cabinet below the altar in the hallway." My sister walks past my duck and me. She takes the soiled folder and heads for the bathroom. "Don't get pricked."

Ate Nadine shuts the door behind her. I remain rooted in place, carrying my duck.

"Let's go, Sab," Pepper says in a soft voice. She gently touches my shoulder. "She'll forgive you and Lawin. Don't worry."

It's not what I'm worried about. "Can I see the photos on your phone?"

CHAPTER TEN
A Picture Speaks a Bajillion Words

"LADIES AND GENTLEMEN, WE ARE done! Am I a genius, or what?"
Pepper holds up the finished duck diaper harness with pride.
It's a complex thing. There's a pocket shaped like a cup, where
a strip of disposable baby diaper will slot into. It's attached to
such a complicated network of intersecting straps, I can't imagine how they'll fit on the duck.

"Definitely a genius." The words leave my mouth without
a second thought. Pepper won't stop hounding me until I say it.
Right now, I have better things to worry about than stroking
her ego.

Like, for example, this photo of an organizational chart entitled "Drug Trade in Pignatelli."

"Ha!" Pepper smirks. She then spreads the harness straps on her lap. "Okay, let's try this out. Can you hand me Lawin?"

"I don't get it. Why does Ate Nadine have to interview Dad's old doctor?" I tear my eyes away from Pepper's phone and meet hers. "There are so many doctors Ate can interview. And I'm sure they're nicer than this man."

"You've asked me that same question all morning. My answer hasn't changed—I don't know. Maybe your sister likes talking to grouchy people. That's very likely, actually. If you're not going to help me out, just paint or something. You've been doing nothing but staring at those photos. They're not going to miraculously tell us why your sister hates your papa." Pepper sighs aloud, taking Lawin from the lidless plastic box herself. "Ugh. This duck is so heavy."

"But my gut tells me it's all connected!"

"Your gut is wrong. Ate Nadine is investigating illegal activity on her campus. It's got nothing to do with your papa. They are two different things, Sab. We need to focus on *our* mission to reconcile them, not butt in on Ate Nadine's boring assignment. Your birthday is this Sunday, and we just don't have the time to do both." Pepper puts on Lawin's harness, her hands flying across clamps and straps like an expert. "Tah-dah!"

"Wow." It's amazing, really, how she did this. Pepper simply downloaded photos of ducks in diapers, studied how they worked, and somehow managed to design one of her own. But it's not enough to distract me from my worries. "My gut has never been wrong."

"It was very wrong yesterday. Remember how you thought Jepoy was out to get us?" Pepper snorts. "Turns out, he's just a friend of your sister's, helping her with the article."

"Well, I was right about him watching us," I insist, pouting.

"Yeah. But without bad intentions. It's not the same thing, Sab."

"It is—"

CRINGGG!

"That's probably your mama calling." Pepper jerks her thumb to the direction of the study. "Why don't you ask her about this doctor-in-the-purple-center thing, if you're so bothered?"

I roll my eyes as I get off the couch. Pepper just doesn't get it. If Mom and I were Americans, I probably would have been able to initiate a conversation like that easily. But we're not. Respect is a huge thing in our culture. I can't just go demanding answers from my elders.

The phone emits another ring. Before I can even open the door to Mom's office, Ate Nadine comes thundering down the stairs. "I'll get it!"

My sister hurries past me and pushes the door closed. But it doesn't slam shut, staying ajar with enough space to hear what Ate Nadine is saying.

"I thought you said eavesdropping is wrong," Pepper whispers.

I shrug away from her, peering inside the room. Ate Nadine is sitting in Mom's office chair, hidden behind the computer monitor. "Go back to the living room and just wait for me there if this bothers you so much."

Pepper holds up her hands and laughs quietly. "Chill. I'm totally for it."

"Thanks for calling again, Ninong. I can hear you so much better now. My cell phone service really has a bad connection around here," Ate Nadine says to the person on the line. Ninong? I haven't met any of my sister's godfathers. Maybe I did, but I was too young to remember. I wonder which ninong this is.

"Mom's good," my sister continues. "Dad? Uhmm . . . I don't know. That's actually why I wanted to talk to you. Today? Like, now? Sure! Are you still staying at the same house? Okay. I can walk there."

My friend and I exchange excited looks. Whoever this godfather is, he's here now. *And* Ate Nadine is off to meet him somewhere in our neighborhood to discuss Dad. This is the lead Pepper and I have been waiting for!

"I'll be there in five."

As Ate Nadine hangs up, Pepper and I scramble back to the sofa. Its springs groan as we jump on it, startling the duck.

"Quack. Quack. Quack!" Lawin pecks at the harness straps but can't get them off. Pepper's design works, making sure the diaper's secure.

"Not bad," Ate Nadine says as she comes out. She cocks her head at Lawin. "He can stay inside, then."

"QUACK!" The duck lets out another loud, frustrated call.

"If you hadn't pooped on my notes, I'd feel sorry for you," Ate Nadine tells Lawin, chuckling. She gives the duck a pat and heads for the door. "I'm going out. Stay here. Tito Ed will be home soon."

I bounce off the sofa. "Can we go with you?"

"No." Ate Nadine shuts the front door behind her before I can protest.

Well, if my sister is doing something that involves Dad (and I know it does—I heard her say it), I need to be in on it. I'm not taking no for an answer this time.

I grab Lawin off the floor, helping him remove the duck diaper. Thankfully, he hasn't pooped yet.

"Hey!" Pepper protests. "What are you doing? I spent the whole morning making that!"

I ignore Pepper and carry Lawin to the kitchen, where we keep the dog kennel he stays in when he's home alone. "He might hurt himself if we leave him with that thing on," I explain. "He's not used to it yet."

"Did you say *leave*?" Pepper helps me put Lawin in the cage, a smile forming on her lips. "You're not planning on following Ate Nadine and spying on her, are you?"

I feel a twinge of guilt. Ate Nadine hates being spied on. She's a very private person. Which is odd, considering her chosen profession. Journalists don't always respect other people's privacy.

My eyes flicker to the butterfly tattoo on my right hand.

Well, I'm going to be a journalist for today. After all, I might never have another chance to be one.

I jerk my head to the direction of the front door. "You ready?"

"Ohhhhh!" Pepper rubs her hands together, grinning. "This is going to be so fun!"

CHAPTER ELEVEN
Trash Spies

"I TAKE IT BACK. THIS isn't fun. No fun at all," Pepper complains, huffing and puffing as she pedals. "You should have told me to bring my bike."

"You're doing great." I give my friend's shoulder a squeeze. We've been following Ate Nadine on my bicycle. Pepper's the one in control, while I'm standing behind her. It's hard not to fall off a short metal bar protruding from the back wheel. Still, I'm sure it's way harder to pedal the bike with an extra passenger while going up a steep incline. If I attempted to do that, I'd be dead even before my week's up.

Pepper and I don't often frequent this part of the subdivision. The houses are modest and have simple, modern designs.

The old narra trees lining the road form a roof of intertwined branches and leaves. It's pretty much like our street, save for the hilly terrain.

I close my eyes for a moment as a cool breeze touches my face. I'm glad to be able to call this subdivision my home. The neighbors are nice, and accidents are practically nonexistent. It seems so boring compared to the alley near Ate's school, where angry vendors can pelt you with insults and bottles of skin whitener. Still, I love how peaceful it is. I doubt I would last long in that chaotic alley without my sister's protection.

"Thank goodness, she's finally stopping." Pepper pants, pedaling harder.

"I see her." I point to a small space on the sidewalk, between a parked SUV and two huge blue drums full of trash. "We can hide there."

Pepper slows the bike, and I jump off before it gets to a full stop.

"If Ate Nadine enters the house, my pain will be for nothing," Pepper grumbles as she follows me to my spot. The drums of trash have covers, but they still reek of rotten eggs and sour milk. "Ugh. So gross! This better be worth it, Sab."

"It is. Look!"

A tall, bald man joins Ate Nadine outside the red gate. He has a fair complexion and a pair of really small eyes. He's probably about the same age as Dad. "I'm sorry I can't stay with you long, Nadine. Do you want to come in? My mother can entertain you when I leave."

"It's okay, Ninong Greg." Ate Nadine leans her back on the gate. "No need to trouble her."

Ah. Godfather Greg. Dad told me about him. He said this man lives in Canada but occasionally visits his mother here in Manila.

"It's good to be back." The man smiles. "How's your dad?"

As expected, a frown creases my sister's forehead. I can sense her discomfort even from afar. "I haven't really talked to him."

"I figured you wouldn't. Your mom emailed me," he explains. "How long has it been since the funeral?"

"Almost a year." Ate Nadine avoids her godfather's gaze. "I had my suspicions. It's not so hard to get info on the internet, you know. But no one really confirmed it with me. Like, they expected me to just accept it. Then I saw those pictures and . . . stuff. How long has he been like that?"

Not just a year. She hasn't spoken to him in 375 days. One year and ten days since Lola Cordia's death. I've been counting. We have just celebrated her babang-luksa last week. Mom wanted us to have the prayers and celebration at Dad's resort, but of course Ate Nadine refused. So we just said the prayers with Daddy and Wendell on video call and had dinner at some fancy restaurant.

But wait. What pictures? What "stuff"?

"You need to talk to your father, anak," Ninong Greg says, referring to my sister as "my child." "Christopher's a good man. He was young when he had you. He didn't know what he was doing—"

"He and Mom were twenty-seven when they had me. He should have known better." Ate Nadine takes a deep breath. "It ruined our family. And he didn't even have the guts to tell me. He owed me an explanation, but he still couldn't tell me even when I confronted him with the pictures. I just want the truth, Ninong Greg. Is that too much to ask?"

Truth? *What* truth? Ate Nadine can't mean Dad being sick. Mom said it was the reason why they couldn't see eye to eye. Then Dad got well, but it was too late for them. Is it possible that's not true? Mom wouldn't have lied to me, would she?

I meet Pepper's gaze. She shrugs, as clueless as I am.

Ninong Greg puts a hand on my sister's shoulder. "I'm sorry. I should have helped your mother more. I should have been there for you more."

"It's not your fault." Ate Nadine assures him with a smile. Even from where I'm squatting, I can see how forced it is. "It's nobody's fault but Dad's."

What *is* Dad's fault? Ate Nadine can't be talking about the time Dad had to recover from his medical condition. Depression. I searched about it online. Dad had a mental illness. But the websites also said it isn't anyone's fault. Surely, Ate Nadine knows that?

"Anak, I know it's hard to forgive him, but he's still your father. He had a condition. Does Romeo Gamelon still live here? He used to play basketball with us in the inter-subdivision tournament. Rom and your dad were tight way back. They were already in the partying scene when I met them. Maybe he can help you better with the answers you seek. I haven't been . . . I should have been in touch with you and your dad more. I'm so sorry."

"Your dad played basketball?" Pepper mouths at me, her eyes wide.

I shrug. It's no big deal. Mom said basketball in the Philippines is a thing dads and titos do to bond. I'm more interested in this Romeo Gamelon.

"Don't worry about it, Ninong. Really," says Ate Nadine. "When are you leaving? Mom would love to catch up with you. She'll be back next week."

My face falls. I was hoping Mom would change her mind, cut her Singapore trip short, and fly here in time for my birthday. I guess my turning eleven isn't that important to her.

"I'll be here for a month." Ninong Greg smiles. "How's your little sister?"

"She's okay. The usual." Ate Nadine shrugs. "Honestly, I think she needs to use the internet less. Sab asks questions way too often."

Ninong Greg laughs. "Sounds exactly like you when you were eleven."

My eyes narrow. I'm liking this Ninong Greg less and less. I am so not like Ate.

A snort escapes Pepper's nose, and she covers her mouth to hide her laughter. I shoot her a warning look. She holds her hands high in surrender, bumping a dirty cup off the drum's cover.

Ate Nadine and her godfather turn to our direction.

Oh no.

Before they catch us, Pepper and I flatten ourselves against the dirty sides of the SUV. We slide down, our backs wiping the car's dust like a rag.

"Nothing to worry about. It must be a cat," Ninong Greg explains. "My mother likes feeding the strays that come here. I'm sorry, anak, but I must go. Dinner soon?"

Pepper and I let out huge sighs of relief. They didn't see us!

"Yes, Ninong." Ate Nadine smiles, nodding. "I'll tell Mom."

My sister gives the bald man a peck on the cheek and leaves as he gets back to his house. Ate Nadine's figure grows smaller and smaller as she walks farther away, eventually disappearing around the corner.

My legs buckle, and I slide all the way down to the dirty cement sidewalk. I spread my legs out to stretch. "Ow."

"Don't worry. Spies don't always succeed in their missions." Pepper settles on the patch of grass in front of me. "We'll get better intel next time."

Ugh. Pepper's "spy lingo" is getting on my nerves. She's

watching way too many reruns of *Chuck* on repeat. "It's not a bust," I say.

"It's not?"

"We have a name." I stand up and dust off my butt. "Ate Nadine might not think he's important enough, but let's find out more about this Romeo Gamelon."

CHAPTER TWELVE
Who Is Romeo Gamelon?

THERE'S JUST ONE PROBLEM.

"How are we going to find Romeo Gamelon?" I kick off my flip-flops and crawl onto my bed. The fairy lights hanging on my headboard rattle at the movement. "There could be thousands of people sharing the same name on the internet. And Dad brought his old yearbooks to Pililia with him when he left."

"You really need to learn how to put the harness on this feathery monster, Sab." Pepper's hands are flying all over Lawin as she puts on his bird diaper. The duck lets out a frustrated quack. "Learn to live with that, or you're staying outside.

Ow! Stop biting me. It was Sab's idea to leave you. Get mad at *her*, not me."

"It's not as if you didn't want to go. You wanted to play CIA agent too." I spread my arms wide and stare at the ceiling. "Do you think there's an online version of Dad's yearbook?"

"There isn't. Mama said the internet they had back in high school was so slow it took twenty bajillion years to download a single picture." Pepper lets go of Lawin. The angry duck gives her one last nip before waddling off to his favorite spot under my desk. "We'll search anyway. Where's your tablet? My battery level is at two percent."

"It's under my sketchpad." I crawl to the foot of the bed as Pepper gets the gadget from my desk. She settles below me, leaning her back on the bed so I can look over her shoulder as she logs on to my account.

Pepper pulls up the browser, and her eyes narrow. "'Black butterfly'? Seriously, Sab? I told you to stop worrying about it. Reading these weird articles isn't going to do you any good."

My hand shoots out from behind her, exiting the browser tabs. "This is a terrible idea. We won't find anything about him online."

"Stop being so negative." Pepper pulls the tablet away from me. She types "Romeo Gamelon," and presses the Search button. "Old people like posting stuff on social media. I'm sure we'll find something about him."

A hundred results come up. I was expecting thousands, but I guess "Romeo Gamelon" isn't a very common name.

Pepper taps the first result. It takes us to a website full of house pictures.

Romeo Gamelon, real estate agent

"Too old." I shake my head, reaching behind Pepper to swipe the page back to the search results. "If he went to high school with Dad, they're probably the same age. He'll have to be like, forty, or something."

I tap on the next result. The link brings us to an article from the *Manila Daily Journal*, Ate Nadine's paper. It's accompanied by the picture of a guy who's supposed to be Romeo Gamelon.

Romeo Gamelon tops bar exams

The Philippine Organization for Lawyers has released the results of the bar exams today . . .

"Too young." Pepper frowns, swiping the screen left. "And he looks too serious to be BFFs with your dad."

"True." This particular Romeo Gamelon was probably just a baby when Dad took part in that inter-subdivision basketball tournament. "Oh, wait. Look at this—" I point at the tablet screen.

The Struggle:

A Photo Series on Recovery by New York–based Filipino American photographer Romeo Gamelon. The Makati Museum for Creative Arts, Makati City.

The art blog features an interview with Romeo Gamelon, where he talks about being Filipino American. He shares his experiences growing up in the Philippines, the hardships he endured on his journey of recovery, and going on adventures taking pictures for international magazines. The article also includes a photograph of him.

Romeo Gamelon has small eyes and a goatee, kind of like Dad's, but it's thinner and sleeker. His skin is black and has a nice sheen—it reminds me of an obsidian stone. His hair is very short, so much shorter than my pixie cut. It's more like the hairstyle military men are required to have.

But, best of all, this Romeo Gamelon looks like he's about the same age as Dad. "This is him," I say.

"I agree. Tomorrow's the last day of his exhibit, and he's going to be there for an open forum with reporters and guests." Pepper tilts her head to face me. "Are you sure about this, Sab? You might be digging up things that are better left alone."

I roll over on the bed, closing my eyes. The springs of the mattress groan as Pepper joins me. I feel her shoulder next to mine.

"If the Butterfly's appearance really is a warning," she continues, "wouldn't you rather have good thoughts about your papa? Like, remember him the way you've always known him? You're worrying about bad stuff that might not even exist. We can just do something fun, you know. Go on food trips. Visit an amusement park. Have a picnic. Go to the beach."

Pepper is right, of course. It would be easy to just let this go and leave it be. But this is my dad we're talking about. My family. It's just not that easy.

I want to know if I'm doing the right thing. Is it worth spending my last days trying to get my sister to make peace with Dad? Ate Nadine sounded really hurt about something. Having my birthday at Dad's resort seems too shallow a reason for them to make peace.

"I need this, Pepper." I lean my head on my best friend's

shoulder. "I know it seems impossible, but I can't die not even trying to help them work things out. I just can't leave this hanging. I can't let this be my unfinished business."

"Okay. I'll be with you no matter what you decide." Pepper takes my hand and gives it a squeeze. "We do have to overcome one major obstacle."

"What?"

Pepper sighs loudly. "Your sister. She is so not going to like it when she learns about the person we want to meet."

CHAPTER THIRTEEN
The Metro Manila Rail Transit

THURSDAY

IT WAS SURPRISINGLY EASY TO convince Ate Nadine to go to Makati, Metro Manila's business district. Pepper and I didn't even have to lie. We told her we wanted to visit the Makati Museum for Creative Arts, and she agreed without any protests. Maybe she had something to do there for her assignment, like that time when I got a haircut. Or maybe she just wanted to take a break. Of course, we didn't mention we wanted to see Romeo Gamelon and his exhibit.

I feel like we're lying by not telling the whole truth. But it's a white lie that needed to be done. It doesn't make me feel better, but I'm dying anyway. What do I have to lose with one little white lie?

What I didn't count on, though, is the fact that Ate Nadine can't use her car. I totally forgot that every Thursday, cars with plate numbers ending seven and eight aren't allowed on the major roads of Metro Manila, particularly in Makati City. Mom, who's an urban planner, explained that keeping some cars off the streets certain days from 7 a.m. to 7 p.m. is a way to help relieve traffic congestion. So, unless Ate Nadine was willing to risk a ticket (she isn't, obviously), we have to commute by train.

Tito Ed dropped us off at the station on his way to work at the police headquarters. It didn't take long for us to reach the Santolan-Annapolis station of the MRT—the Metro Manila Rail Transit. Getting on the train is a different story.

The place is like a wet market. It's noisy, and it's crowded. It reeks of body odor, pollution, and random food smells. The morning sun doesn't make things easier, turning the station into a giant pizza oven. The humidity is so bad, my skin is as sticky as a Post-it. The station's ceiling fans do nothing to ease the heat. Waiting passengers must use whatever they have on hand to cool themselves.

"This is such a bad idea," I grumble, craning my neck in search of Ate Nadine. It's no use. My sister is somewhere in the thick crowd of people, battling her way to the ticket booth. The line, I'm horrified to see, snakes all the way down the station entrance—a feat I only thought possible at a Taylor Swift concert. "I take it back. We should just take a taxi."

"We're already here." Pepper looks at the security guard standing beside us. Ate Nadine promised the man fifty pesos to watch over us while we wait. "It'll get better when we're on the train."

My eyes narrow. How does she know? Just like me, Pepper's never been on the MRT before. Ate Nadine asked us if we prefer to ride a taxi, but the train sounded more fun. After all, I only ever see it from the highway. Mom once said we are lucky we can afford to avoid taking the MRT—as if the train is a last-resort kind of thing.

Well, if I'm dying, I might as well try something that's different, right?

Wrong.

This MRT idea is a bad idea that's becoming badder by the second. I can totally understand why Mom never considered it an option for me.

"You look like Ate Nadine when you make that face. Chill out. It's part of the experience. If you back out now, you'll waste the time Ate Nadine spent lining up for our tickets," Pepper says. She has a good point. My sister will be furious if I say I changed my mind. Pepper purses her lips. "Focus, Sab. We're here to find out stuff about your sister and your papa."

Through the window, I see the EDSA freeway below. Cars and buses are moving at a snail's pace. Some honk their horns, while idling jeepneys blast loud rap music. Above the noise, a conductor shouts their routes to passing pedestrians.

I have to be honest. I worry what Romeo Gamelon will say. Part of me wants to let it be, to go back home and just enjoy my remaining days if I really am to die. But I don't want to end up like that man in the Butterfly article, to die sad and desperate because of unfinished business.

As I take a deep breath, I accidentally inhale a cloud of dust and end up in coughing fit.

"Do you need your inhaler?" Pepper thumps my back, reaching for my bag. "I'll get it."

"I'm fine."

Pepper brings out my inhaler from my backpack anyway, forcing it into my hand. "Take it."

I put the puffer in my mouth, inhaling the bitterness of asthma medicine. It relieves the tension in my chest but not the enormous worry building in my gut.

"Are you okay, Sab?" Ate Nadine appears in front of us. There are so many people, we didn't notice her coming. "Can you breathe?"

All I can do is nod. I really don't want to inhale smoke again.

"It's the pollution. I made her take it just in case. The dust is unbelievable," Pepper says, wrinkling her nose. Pepper puts the inhaler back in my bag and studies Ate Nadine. "What happened to you?"

My sister's usually miraculous hair sticks out in odd places, like a web woven by a drunken spider. Sweat drenches the front of her shirt. She looks as though she's been through a catfight, or wrestled a lion.

"Don't ask." Ate Nadine winces as she gives the security guard fifty pesos. She glances over her shoulder and gives us a couple of plastic cards. "Your tickets. Don't lose them. I went through Hell for those."

The MRT ticket reminds me of a credit card but more decorative. There's fancy art on one side and a line map showing train stops. It says that from our location, we'll have to go through five stops before reaching our destination, the Ayala station.

I notice Ate Nadine is holding an extra card. "Who's that for?"

"Over here!" Ate Nadine calls, waving her hand at somebody among the cluster of people at the ticket booth. "I got your ticket."

A familiar, good-looking guy emerges from the crowd. "Hello."

Jepoy.

Or rather, *Kuya* Jepoy. He's really not my brother, but he's older than I am. It's only right to refer to him with respect—even if I did accuse him (without saying it aloud, of course) of being a thug out to hurt my sister.

My worries dissolve. I raise an eyebrow. "Why is he here? Is he going to be our bodyguard again?"

I'm not being rude. I'm curious. What *is* Kuya Jepoy doing here?

Ate Nadine gives me a warning look. "I told you, he's helping me with my article. He's meeting a source for me, since I have to go to this silly museum with you. Now be quiet and be nice."

Before I can say anything else, Ate Nadine is already guiding us through the ticket terminal. She keeps her grip tight so we won't be swept away by the throngs of people eager to board the train.

"I don't get it." Pepper wipes sweat off her brow when we reach the platform. "Why do you have to pay the guard for something that he's supposed to do? Papa says bribery like this can get you arrested."

"Not in the Philippines." Ate Nadine pulls us closer to her, even though it's pointless. Pepper and I aren't going anywhere. There are so many people on the platform we can barely move an inch. "It's not an excuse to perpetuate this culture of corruption, but sometimes, you do what you have to do."

The rails rattle loudly as the train arrives. There's a sound like steam being released, which Ate Nadine says is the MRT's brake system. The car doors open, and everyone hurries in.

"Ate—"

"Hold tight, Sab. Pepper, take my other hand! Jepoy—"

The sealike current of human bodies carries us to the near-est car, separating us from Kuya Jepoy. Before we can enter, an attendant steers us to a different car. He says this one is reserved for women, children, senior citizens, people with disabilities, and "pretty girls" like Pepper. I doubt we'd get such special treat-ment if my friend hadn't been white. Because, in a country of brown-skinned Filipinos, white people "deserve" only the best.

Refusing this privilege would have been the right thing to do. It's not fair to everyone else who is squeezing themselves into the more crowded cars. But like Ate Nadine said, you do what you have to do. I just want to get on the train and leave this horrible station.

"Jepoy! Please text me when you get the medical research. The doctor said he'll leave it with his secretary. Babayaran na lang kita." Ate Nadine calls out that she'll pay him back, as he's ushered to another car.

Kuya Jepoy doesn't get to answer, because the doors finally close. I breathe a huge sigh of relief.

"This isn't so bad—" I turn to face Pepper as a woman's elbow collides with my nose. "Ow!"

"Are you okay?" Ate Nadine tries to examine my face, but she's pinned between a lady and her friend.

"I'm fine, Ate." It's not entirely true. My nose doesn't hurt much, but I feel like I'm going to suffocate to death.

I thought it'd be fun, riding the train like Harry Potter going to Hogwarts. But no. Riding the MRT is one of the worst ideas ever. I should have risked Ate Nadine's ire and backed out when I had the chance.

The train stops, opening its doors for more people to come in.

Really?

"We're now at Ortigas station, Sab," Ate Nadine says, pulling Pepper and me close. More people wedge themselves inside the car. "If you want to take a cab, we'll have to get off at Shaw."

By "Shaw," Ate Nadine means Shaw Boulevard, where the MRT station connects to a mall. According to the map on our ticket, it's the next station coming up.

"Up to you," Pepper mumbles, trying to keep her face away from an old lady's exposed armpit.

Funny. Moments ago, she convinced me not to back out. I don't mean to be petty, but I'm icky, I'm thirsty, and I'm stuck in a train that's more crowded than a can of sardines.

The MRT lurches forward, and I grab hold of the pole to keep my balance.

Unfortunately for Pepper, the force of the train slams her face right into the old lady's armpit. Pepper swings back as she holds the handrail tighter, her face twisted in disgust.

I try to keep a straight face, but Ate Nadine bursts out laughing.

Pepper scowls. The Armpit Lady stares at my sister like she's dangerous and tries to move away from us. It's useless, of course. There are too many people inside, and the most the woman can do is turn her body the other way.

Well, at least now Pepper won't need to worry about armpits landing on her face.

Pepper seems as though she's about to cry—or throw up—any minute now. I don't want her to cry. I *definitely* don't want her to throw up. After all, she's doing this for me, and getting barfed on is gross. I twist to my left to show her my bag. "I have wet wipes in there."

"I don't want wet wipes. Let's get off at the next station, please," Pepper begs. "I can't—"

The train lurches again, harder this time, and Pepper finds herself squished under the woman's armpit once more. Ate Nadine takes hold of me, keeping us both steady.

EEEEEEEE!

For a moment, I think somebody farted. But thankfully, it's just the sound of the train's brakes. "Are we there yet?"

My sister blinks. "No. It's not supposed to—"

A loud chime from the public announcement system interrupts her.

"The MRT is experiencing some technical difficulties," a man's voice explains after introducing himself as the MRT driver. "All passengers are advised to disembark from the train in an orderly fashion. Please present your tickets to the attendants on the platform for credit on your next trip. We apologize for the inconvenience. Magandang umaga po sa inyong lahat."

There's another chime, signaling the end of the driver's message. The doors slide open—right in the middle of the elevated railway.

CHAPTER FOURTEEN
A Woman in Black

"GOOD MORNING, EVERYONE" IS THE worst way for the public announcement to end.

For one, it's noon. For another, they've just made us exit the train on an elevated railway under the searing heat of Manila summer. Worse, the station platform seems so far away that it's like a desert mirage. I just can't see anything good in that.

No one seems to think abandoning the train in the middle of the railway is anything out of the ordinary. Ate Nadine says this happens often, and if I watched the news, I'd know. But I don't really care if it's a normal thing or not. We are so not going to make it to the museum in time to meet Romeo Gamelon.

He'll be gone by the time we get there, unless we somehow manage to teleport from this place.

This *isn't* a minor inconvenience. It's a *disaster.*

On our left side is the train, blue and white with a thin red stripe in the middle. The guardrail on our right is dusty and gray. One false move and you might find yourself splattered on the EDSA freeway below.

Most of the passengers are probably thinking the same thing. We're walking far from the sides, crowding in the middle like the starting line of a marathon.

Well, most of us are anyway. There are a few daredevils near the edge, strolling as if they're in a park and not on an elevated railway.

I'm staying right here in the middle, where it's safe.

"Ate! Don't go so near the edge," I warn, keeping the fear in my voice to a minimum.

My sister just throws me an angry look. She doesn't stray far, but she continues to talk to Kuya Jepoy and ignores me.

Seriously? I know I'm the one who wanted to go to Makati. Maybe I should have remembered Ate's car can't be used on Thursday, but it's not my fault the MRT stalled.

"Ahh-tehhhh!" I lick my dry lips. I'm whining like a brat, I know. But I can't help myself. "I'm hungry."

Ate Nadine finally stops talking. She turns to look at me, her face in a scowl. "Be quiet, Sab. Your whining is grating on my ears worse than fingernails on a blackboard."

This is one of those moments when I don't appreciate her talent for words. I cross my arms over my chest and say the first thing that comes to mind. "You're so mean!"

"Ohh-kay. You both need to chill." Pepper steps in between us. "Who wants some taffy? I still have some—"

"Oh, you be quiet too!"

Ate Nadine marches on, staying as near the guardrail as possible. Away from me.

"Talk about cranky." Pepper snorts. "Somebody better feed the dragon before it burns us all."

Kuya Jepoy approaches Ate Nadine, but she shrugs his hand away. Then he says something, and the scowl on my sister's face disappears. Whatever he said, it definitely calmed her down. They're deep in conversation before long. My sister's frown remains on her face, but it's no longer angry. It's the same frown she wears whenever she's thinking, or something's bothering her.

I quicken my steps. "Let's get closer. I want to hear what they're saying."

"I don't know, Sab," says Pepper. She pops a taffy into her mouth and chews like it's the most important candy in the world. "This whole spying-on-Ate-Nadine thing . . . It seems wrong."

My eyes narrow. Pepper is having guilty feelings *now*?

"Hear me out," she continues, holding up her hands. "I just think you're getting too obsessed about your papa's involvement in Ate Nadine's assignment. Aren't you worried about the trouble you'll be in if she finds out you've been spying on her every chance you get?"

"That's not what you said last time." I pout.

"Yeah." Pepper twirls a lock of brown hair around her finger. "I'm your best friend, Sab. I'll support you all the way, but . . . I don't know. Just think about it?"

"I will." But not today. Right now, I need to hear what Ate Nadine and Kuya Jepoy are saying. I take a puff of my inhaler and quicken my steps. "Can you hurry up a bit?"

My friend lets out a long sigh. "All right."

"Is this source good?" Ate Nadine asks Kuya Jepoy.

"Yeah." He nods. "The boy's a regular—I see him in the

alley often. He's willing to talk as long as you keep his identity secret."

"I can do that."

"And he wants it to be in a public place. No cameras."

"Of course."

Kuya Jepoy falls silent, staring straight ahead. "I've been meaning to ask . . ." He clears his throat. "Why are you doing this? I know it's your dream to intern for a national paper, but this assignment . . . It seems different."

"Someone needs to do something about the drug problem in Pignatelli, Jepoy." Ate Nadine's lips form a grim line. "It ruins lives. Families. My report is going to help the police bring these sellers to justice."

"Okay."

"It's personal." My sister huffs. "You of all people should understand."

A Goth-looking woman in a black shirt and black jeans bumps into an old man in front of me. "Watch it!" he protests.

How rude.

"I can respect that." Kuya Jepoy nods. "I owe you a lot. I'll help you any way I can, but be careful. I might not be around to protect you all the time."

Ate Nadine smiles. Her expression reminds me of the time when an ex-girlfriend sent her a huge bouquet of roses for her sixteenth birthday. My sister tucks her hair behind an ear like she's embarrassed. "Anyway, is the source a student—"

Hmm . . .

"Your sister is the most un-romantic human being on the planet." Pepper snorts, interrupting my thoughts. "I should know. I get forced to watch Mama's teleserye drama all the time. Sab? Yo, Sab!"

I ignore Pepper. There's something not right about the woman in black. She's walking strangely, zigzagging on the train tracks.

My heart drops to my stomach, like something bad is about to happen.

The woman is dangerously close to the edge now and looks like she's about to puke.

Going near the railing scares me, but I think she needs help. I take a deep breath. If today is the day, I might as well use some of my remaining time to help someone else *not* die.

I quicken my step and stop by the woman's side. "Ma'am, are you okay?"

"What's going on?" Pepper comes up behind me.

The woman staggers, then her legs buckle. Luckily, I catch her just as she loses her balance, falling right on top of me. Pepper tries to grab the woman's arm, but it's too late. The woman and I stumble backward onto the railway.

"Oh!" My head lands just an inch from the hard, metal train tracks. I feel sick at the thought that falling just one inch to the left would have been my end.

"Saklolo! Tulungan nyo po kami," I call on to the passing MRT passengers. "Help! Please help us."

"Sab!"

Ate Nadine and Kuya Jepoy hurry to my side. My pulse is hammering so fast I can hardly speak. "She . . ."

The woman in black throws up near the railing and slumps to the ground. She stops moving.

"Oh no." I gasp. "Is she dead?"

Is this the death the Butterfly warned me about?

My legs feel weak at the thought, and I reach out to the person beside me.

"Take it easy," says Ate Nadine, putting an arm around my shoulders. Her body spray of strawberries and cream is a refreshing smell compared to the pollution and stink of the

MRT. "Let's lay her down near the train where there's shade. Jepoy—"

Kuya Jepoy carries the woman as though she weighs nothing at all.

"Is she okay?" I look over Ate Nadine's shoulder. The woman's face is pasty white, but it's not like Pepper's complexion. It's more like the blood had been drained out of her face.

"I'm a doctor." A woman stops and kneels beside the Goth lady, feeling her pulse. "What happened?"

"She was walking like she was drunk, then just collapsed," I manage to croak.

"Yeah," Pepper says. "Then she threw up."

"Do you have water?" The doctor touches the Goth lady's forehead. "Face towel?"

"Water, yes." Pepper looks at me, and I nod. She gives my water bottle to the woman, then waves her pink Hello Kitty hankie. "Will this do?"

The doctor wets the cloth with water and places it on the woman's forehead. The woman stirs. "Try to drink if you can, miss."

"What happened to her?" Ate Nadine asks.

"Heat exhaustion. She'll be okay." She gives Pepper a smile. "Thanks to you."

Seriously? The green monster (not to be mistaken as Pepper's ugly clay art) is screaming inside me.

Of course Pepper gets the credit, she's the pretty one. I'm too brown to be acknowledged for anything as long as she's around.

"Not me." Pepper pushes me forward. "I just helped Sab help her."

Guilt washes over me. My friend isn't like most people. She wouldn't take credit for something she didn't do. It's just the way she is, and I love her for it.

"Well, Sab. You just saved this woman." The doctor smiles at me. "If I were your mom, I'd be very proud of you."

My sister starts clapping, and then Pepper. Then Kuya Jepoy, then the doctor. Soon, everyone around us is putting their hands together in a round of applause.

For me. They're clapping *for me.*

"Way to go, Sab!" Pepper hoots. "My best friend's a hero!"

Hero seems a bit much, but I do like the sound of that. I grin. Things might not go the way I expected them to, and this will probably be the first and the last time it'll ever happen, but it sure feels good to be a hero for the day.

I'm Sabrina Florence Dulce, savior of dehydrated strangers.

With that, I take a bow, and the MRT passengers clap even louder.

CHAPTER FIFTEEN
Kare-kare and Dirty Ice Cream

IN MOMENTS LIKE THESE, I'M so glad I'm not allergic to peanuts.

This kare-kare must be life's way of rewarding my heroism, bringing me to this carinderia. Because this canteen has the best kare-kare ever.

Swimming among the orange peanut sauce are beef chunks and pieces of ox tripe with melt-in-your-mouth texture. It also has a generous amount of soft eggplants, string beans, and pechay greens. The peanut sauce isn't too thick, nor is it too thin. It's the perfect sauce on a cup of steamed rice. Add a dash of their sweet-and-spicy shrimp paste, and you've got a saucy, savory, and slightly sweet combination that's like heaven on earth.

I wolf down the last of my kare-kare and rice, licking the

back of my spoon. The Butterfly's prediction could come true at this very moment, and I wouldn't mind.

"If you start licking your plate, I'm disowning you," Ate Nadine quips. She's far from being finished with her own food. Still, it seems like she's had enough to improve her mood.

Cling! Cling! Cling! There's a loud tinkling coming from the street.

"Ice cream!" Pepper pushes her empty plate away and bounces off the stool. She turns her begging eyes across the table to Ate Nadine. "Let's get some before an angry woman pelts us with skin whiteners again."

Ate Nadine rolls her eyes, but nonetheless she brings out a small wad of cash. I reach for it, but she hands it to Kuya Jepoy instead. "Don't let them have more than three small cones of dirty ice cream each. And stay away from the street. Sab's too oblivious; she might get run over by a car."

If Mom were here, she probably wouldn't let me have dirty ice cream. When she was a kid, "dirty ice cream" really *was* dirty until children started getting sick. The government has created laws to ensure these treats are made in clean conditions, but the name has stuck. It's still called dirty ice cream, even if it's safe to eat.

Well, Mom's not here now. She doesn't have to know I had a cone. Or two.

"I am not oblivious." I pout. I don't really know what *oblivious* means, but it sounds eerily similar to that Harry Potter spell that erases someone's memory. Whatever it is, it doesn't sound like a compliment.

Anyway, it's not my fault I don't know how to cross a busy street. Mom doesn't let me commute on my own, and cars in a gated subdivision like ours follow an unspoken rule to stop if they see kids on the street. It's not as if I ever have to worry about getting run over or anything.

I follow Kuya Jepoy and Pepper out of the canteen, where an elderly man is pushing a wooden ice cream cart a few yards away. He's about to round the corner when Kuya Jepoy lets out a piercing whistle, raising his hand. The vendor turns his cart and heads back our way.

"Thanks." If not for Kuya Jepoy, Pepper and I would have had to call the dirty ice cream vendor the hard way—by chasing him down.

Kuya Jepoy just smiles. He's not much of a talker, and that's coming from someone who's on the quiet side.

"Wow," Pepper exclaims. "How did you do that? Every

time I try to whistle, it comes out like this—" She puts her index and middle fingers in her mouth and blows. No piercing whistle comes out, except for a farting sound and a shower of spit that lands on my arm.

"Pepper!" I take a step back, rubbing my arm on my shirt. "Gross."

Pepper sticks her tongue out at me.

"You'll get it, eventually." Kuya Jepoy chuckles. It's surprisingly comforting—low, rumbling, and contagious.

The dirty ice cream vendor pulls up in front of us by the sidewalk. Pepper looks over his shoulder as he opens the metal canisters embedded in the wooden cart. "What flavors do you have in there, sir?"

"Ube, chocolate, and cheese," the vendor answers, readying a small cone and his ice cream scooper. "Ten pesos per cone."

"I'll have a cone with both chocolate and ube." Pepper grimaces. "No cheese, please."

"Just cheese for me." I love cheese ice cream. I don't know why Pepper hates it. It's sweet, creamy, and salty at the same time. I gave my tiny cone a lick. The scoops are no bigger than a golf ball, the perfect size for a quick dessert or afternoon snack. Hmm . . . *Delicious.*

Kuya Jepoy hands the vendor twenty pesos, just enough for two.

I frown. "You're not getting any?"

He shakes his head. Kuya Jepoy brings out a wad of gum instead, unwraps it, and pops it in his mouth.

"I've seen one of those." Pepper licks her ice cream, blending the purple ube with the brown chocolate. "Papa uses it to quit smoking. You smoke?"

"Used to," Kuya Jepoy says with a grimace. "It was really hard to quit."

Pepper stops eating. She stares the older boy straight in the eye. "Papa also said smoking will destroy your lungs."

"Yeah," agrees Kuya Jepoy. "He's not wrong."

"Some of Ate Nadine's classmates smoke at coffee shops," I say, remembering what my sister told me. "She said it's an icky way to deal with stress."

"I wouldn't know." Kuya Jepoy shrugs. "I've never been to college."

"Oh no. He's getting away. I want another one!" Pepper pops the last of her cone into her mouth. She takes the money from Kuya Jepoy, who whistles again for the vendor to stop.

He does, but this time, he doesn't make an effort to turn back. Pepper rolls her eyes and jogs after him.

The ice cream vendor probably got bored hearing us talk.

"Wouldn't you want to? Go to college, I mean?" I swallow the last of my cone, covering my mouth to quiet my burp. "Ate Nadine says San Jose Pignatelli offers scholarships. Like, you go to college but you don't have to pay to attend the classes."

"Yep. She told me the same thing," Kuya Jepoy says with a kind smile. Up close, I notice he has a chipped tooth. "Your sister has a great heart. I should know. I have five sisters."

"Oh, wow. Five?" I wince. Imagine, living with five duplicates of Ate Nadine. "Are they all your ates too?"

"I'm their kuya. Our youngest is almost as old as you." He touches a bracelet on his wrist. It's pretty, made out of wooden beads with little carvings on them. I'm sure Dad would like it if he saw it. "I miss them. They're in the province with my lola. Farm life suits them better."

"Is your mom here in Manila with you?" I hope he doesn't think I'm being nosy.

Kuya Jepoy shakes his head. "My parents are with the Lord now. I live with my tito—well, I used to. I live alone now."

"I'm sorry." And I really am. It must be so hard to lose both parents. I'll be very sad if something bad happens to my mom or any of my three dads. "Sorry about your tito too."

"Oh, he's still alive."

"What do you mean?" It's odd, the way he says it.

"My tito made this for me. It was his 'apology' gift." Kuya Jepoy studies his bracelet. "He made it while in prison."

I gasp. "What?"

"Sorry, sometimes I forget my story can be a lot to take." Kuya Jepoy laughs in a kind way. "I was sixteen when Lola and I decided I should find a job in Manila. We all thought my uncle was just a welder, as he said he was. But he was doing illegal things. Then a job went bad. He got caught, and it landed him in jail. It's hard to be alone, but it's okay. I learned to be independent."

"What!"

"It's all good. His neighbor took me in. Gave me a job at her internet café—she's like a mother to me." Kuya Jepoy ruffles my hair. "I'm not rich. I don't have a college education. But I have a job, family, and friends. Not many people can say that. Most are too poor to eat."

Well, whatever Dad did, I hope it's not as terrible as what Kuya Jepoy's uncle did to him. Which reminds me: "Is there another way to Makati that's not the MRT?"

Kuya Jepoy nods. "We can take a jeepney, but that'll take too long, and you might not last in the heat. I can get us a cab, if your sister is okay with it."

"No, I'm not okay with that idea at all." Ate Nadine appears between Kuya Jepoy and me, her hands on her hips. "It's time to go home, Sab. We've had enough adventure today. Where's Pepper?"

"Here!" My friend joins us with another cone of brown-and-purple ice cream. "Where are we off to next?"

Ate Nadine says "home" at the same time I utter "Makati." Her eyes are like lasers zapping me to pieces, but I don't flinch.

"Aww, come on. It's not every day the girls get to go out like this." Kuya Jepoy grins at my sister. "Where's your sense of adventure?"

"I left it on the MRT railway," Ate Nadine hisses like an angry cat. "I just want to go home and take a long bath."

"Please, Ate," I beg, not bothering to widen my eyes like Pepper does. I'll just look like a scared little owl anyway. From the corner of my eye, Kuya Jepoy flags down a taxi. "I really want to go to the museum. It's been a long time since I've seen great art on display. I need the inspiration, Ate. Today's the last day and—"

"Arghhh! I hate it when you do that. It's so manipulative." Ate Nadine holds up her hands in surrender. "Dad shouldn't have taught you to be so obsessed with art. This museum better be worth it. Jepoy, can you—"

"Already done," Kuya Jepoy says as he theatrically opens the door of a taxicab for my sister. "Step right in, ladies. We're off to the amazing urban jungle that is Makati!"

Pepper and I do as we're told without hesitation. Finally, we'll figure out what happened between Dad and Ate Nadine. And maybe, just maybe, we'll still have time to fix it—whatever it is.

CHAPTER SIXTEEN
The Struggle

I'VE BEEN TO MAKATI A few times with Mom—and even Dad and Wendell—but we always went around in our own car. All I can remember was the bumper-to-bumper traffic, limited parking areas, and the tall buildings.

The traffic's still terrible, and the parked cars on the side of the roads make the streets seem like they're more crowded than they really are. So Ate Nadine had us walk the remaining blocks to the museum from the waiting shed. "If that taxi meter goes any higher," she said, "I'll be so broke that we'll have to walk all the way back to Quezon City."

Thankfully, walking when it's almost evening isn't as terrible as it is in the morning or at noon. The tall structures protect us from the sun like giant umbrellas. The few rays that peek through turn the building walls and tinted glass windows red orange. There are a few trees and potted plants here and there, but it's mostly concrete, glass, and steel.

Makati lives up to its reputation as Manila's main business district—modern, professional, and fast-paced. It's beautiful in its own way, but I'd still choose the safety and calm of our subdivision over this city.

We pass by a few banks, a convenience store, and a bunch of office lobbies where employees come and go. There's even a specialty art shop. The gorgeous rows of oil pastel crayons tempt me to go in, but I resist. The museum is open until six o'clock—we only have an hour left before it closes. Romeo Gamelon's interview was scheduled for four o'clock, so it's possible he's still around answering questions or something.

I hope.

"We're here!" Pepper points to a two-story building. It's like a dwarf compared to the tall structures around it. Up front, there's a concrete sign and an announcement board.

Museo para sa Malikhaing Sining ng Makati.

Below the seal of Makati City, it says:

The Makati Museum for Creative Arts

is proud to present

The Struggle: A Photo Series on Recovery

by New York–based Filipino American photographer Romeo Gamelon

"Romeo Gamelon? How did you—" Ate Nadine glares at Pepper and me. "Who told you about Romeo Gamelon? Did Dad put you up to this? Or have you two been spying on me?"

I turn to Pepper, my heart hammering in my chest. There's no getting out of this. We need to come clean. "Well—"

"Of course not," Pepper says with a wave of her hand. "Why do you always think everything is about you?"

Ate Nadine's eyes narrow dangerously, but Kuya Jepoy steps in and touches her elbow. "Nadine," he says in a low voice, calming and rumbling. My pulse slows down before it reaches asthma levels. I can see Ate Nadine's defenses melting away. Well, not so much. Maybe a little. "Let them explain."

Pepper gives me a pointed look.

I sigh. I *hate* lying, but I need answers. This is my only chance to speak to Romeo Gamelon. I'll deal with my guilt later. "We saw a poster about his exhibit on social media." It's true. The announcement graphic *was* posted on social media.

"Yeah. His exhibit sounded like a culturally enriching experience. We just had to go and see it!" says my friend, happily ushering us to the museum entrance. Ate Nadine looks like she's having second thoughts. Then she rolls her eyes and follows Pepper and me. She pays for our entrance fee, and finally, we're inside.

My heartbeat quickens again. Not with fear or stress this time, but excitement. Well, mostly excitement.

I wipe my clammy hands on my shorts. Hopefully, Ate Nadine's godfather speaks the truth—Romeo Gamelon will have the answers we seek. He will know why Ate Nadine hates Dad so much.

The halls of the Makati Museum for Creative Arts remind me of the hallway in the main house of Lola Cordia's resort. But bigger and longer. The walls on both my left and right are full of paintings and photographs from artists all over the Philippines.

Soon, a black sign with white text bearing THE STRUGGLE in cursive comes into view. It leads us to a room at the far end of the empty hallway. My heart sinks. The open forum with the artist definitely looks over now.

Even so, I take a step forward. Romeo Gamelon could still be here.

Then a man in a blue polo shirt and black slacks steps forward. "Miss, bawal bata dito." He blocks our path, saying that children aren't allowed here. "Over thirteen only."

Pepper and I exchange looks. That wasn't on the gallery poster. It never said we couldn't see it!

"Oh well," Ate Nadine says in a chirpy voice. I frown. She can at least pretend to be disappointed for me. "Time to go home, then!"

Pepper straightens her back, pointing to the sign. "It says here, 'PG-13.' That means 'parental guidance,' not restricted to kids below thirteen."

"These two seem too young to be your parents." The man smirks, flipping his long black hair. "Listen, white girl. I've been watching galleries for this museum before you were even born. I know what PG-13 means."

I give Pepper a look. She doesn't have to sound so bossy. While it's okay most of the time, not everyone will let her get away with things just because she's white. Colonial mentality (as Ate Nadine calls it) may be the case for most people, but there are folks like this man who won't put up with it. For some weird reason, I'm glad he didn't. I respect him for it.

My friend pouts, crossing her arms over her chest. She's obviously not used to getting a response like this. Ate Nadine simply shrugs—I know she'd be happy to turn away and go home. But Kuya Jepoy gives me an encouraging nod.

It's now up to me.

"My mom is in Singapore, and my dad is in Rizal," I explain, staring at the man straight in the eyes without being disrespectful. "Ate Nadine is my guardian. She's eighteen. Kuya Jepoy is—" I turn to the older boy.

"Twenty-one," he answers, giving the man a small, disarming smile. "We're both old enough to explain things to the girls if need be."

The man adjusts his tie and clears his throat. "Well . . ."

"Sige na po, manong. Papasukin nyo na po kami." I clasp my hands together like I'm praying. Unlike Pepper, I can't do a "cute kitty look," but maybe my pleas (or begging) will be convincing enough. "Please, sir. Please let us in. I'm an artist too, but I've been having difficulty getting inspired. Seeing great art will help me a lot to get over that funk."

"Very well." The man sighs so loudly it echoes in the gallery. "It's not every day I see children interested in the arts as much as you are."

"Thank you!" I squeal, giving the man a quick hug. "You are *awesome*."

"Yes, yes." The man steps back, straightening the crumples I made on his shirt. But I can see he's pleased. "Go on in."

We do, and the first photograph greets us. It's entitled *Life Will Go On*. It sounds like a crappy love song, but the image featured in the photograph is far from being romantic.

A dead dog in the gutter, with cars and people passing by. Yup. Definitely not romantic.

"Oh, wow." Pepper's blue eyes widen. "That's . . ."

"Horrible," I say. Cruel. How can these people walk by with this poor little dog dead in the gutter?

Ate Nadine raises an eyebrow. "I thought you said you were looking forward to this exhibit?"

"We were." Pepper nods. "But we didn't think it would be about . . . *this*."

"Didn't you read the gallery description?" Ate Nadine frowns. "You know what . . . Maybe this isn't such a good idea, after all. Let's just go home, Sab."

Pepper and I read the small text inscription under the exhibit title.

THE STRUGGLE: A PHOTO SERIES ON RECOVERY IS ROMEO GAMELON'S FIRST FORAY INTO EXPRESSIVE PHOTO REPRESENTATION. HIS IMAGE ESSAYS AIM TO CAPTURE THE EXPERIENCES OF DIFFERENT PEOPLE WHO ENDURED SUBSTANCE ABUSE BY THEMSELVES, THE ONES THEY'VE HURT, AND THOSE WHO HELPED THEM RECOVER.

"Wow. That's actually pretty cool." This exhibit won't be a walk in a park, that's for sure. Hopefully, the artist shows up soon and we won't have to stay here too long.

Ate Nadine groans, but Kuya Jepoy just laughs.

"Aren't you supposed to explain this to us?" Pepper tilts her head in their direction.

"What else do you need to know?" Ate Nadine snorts. "It's pretty obvious. The dog is dead, but no one cares."

I gasp. "Ate!"

"What?" She shrugs. "I'm a journalist, not an art critic."

"Okay, that's enough." Kuya Jepoy grins. "Let's go see the others."

The rest of the photos aren't so bad. The one with the dog seems to be the only one that's really graphic. The others are more like abstract representations of drug addiction and its effect on other people.

Like this one, *The Downward Spiral*. It shows nothing but an empty staircase, taken from the top. The steps form a tunnel, kind of like looking down into a tornado. "That's intense. The swirling. It's really drawing me in."

"It makes me dizzy." Pepper blinks and rubs her eyes. She moves on to the next photo.

I try not to roll my eyes. Pepper is taking the images literally.

A tall shadow appears on the surface of the photo in front of me. It's Kuya Jepoy. "I get what you mean. It's like you're getting sucked in," he says. "You're falling deeper and deeper, but you have no idea where the bottom is—if there's even a bottom. All you have are fear and uncertainty, but you let yourself fall anyway."

"Like a black hole. There's no other way out but down."

"Yes." Kuya Jepoy nods. "Exactly."

"Sab!" Pepper calls. I turn and find her in front of a photo of a family. "Look at that. Scary!"

Outside the family's living room, right under the window, is a man hiding in the shadows. We can't see his face, but his eyes are wide open and dilated.

But it's not the man in the window I'm drawn to.

It's the family.

"*Isolation*,'" I read the caption. This family on the background shows a young boy celebrating his birthday. The other kids and their parents seem to be happy. The celebrant's mother is smiling, but her eyes are on the wall clock, like she's waiting for someone to arrive. People always look at the clock when they're waiting for someone.

The birthday boy, on the other hand, has his eyes trained on the right of the scene. I can't see what he's looking at exactly, but I'm going to guess it's the door.

You see, I did the exact same thing on my fifth birthday. I waited for Daddy, who promised he wouldn't be late for my party. I blew my candles without him around, kind of like the boy in the picture. Dad came home way after midnight instead.

"Sab." Ate Nadine rests a hand on my shoulder, then gives it a reassuring squeeze. "Do you want to go home?"

I shake my head. "There's more to see."

We move on to the next photo. This time, it features a man and a woman hugging.

"That's so sweet," Pepper says, staring at the photo with a dreamy expression.

Well, "sweet" is one way of looking at it. This image is titled "*Soul Mates*," but with the word *Soul* crossed out. Like, without the soul, just mates. Or maybe the soul is missing.

It's a very appropriate title.

The man in the photo has his eyes closed. He's smiling contently. The woman with the long, messy hair, on the other hand, remains as expressionless as the creepy man in the previous photo. She has red dots on her arms.

My stomach drops. I don't know why, but the woman reminds me so much of my dad. The disheveled look, the seemingly "not there" expression. I close my mouth tightly so I don't throw up.

This is not good.

I grab the hand nearest mine, thinking it's Pepper's. But it's not. Instead, I find myself holding Ate Nadine's hand, and she's staring at me with a frown on her face.

I feel like she's waiting for me to ask something. Honestly, I feel like I need to ask her something. But my brain is too scared to form the words. Not because Ate Nadine will get mad—more like, I'm afraid of the answers I'll get.

"Well, well, well! The attendant wasn't kidding when he said my youngest guests have arrived," a tall Black man with a rumbling voice exclaims. He holds out his hand. "I'm Romeo Gamelon. You can call me Rom."

We introduce ourselves to him. For some reason, we don't tell him our surnames. Even Ate Nadine.

"This woman looks familiar," says Pepper, pointing to the wild-haired lady in the *Soul Mates* image.

"Oh, you like that one? It's my favorite too." Rom smiles, his perfectly white teeth a stark contrast to his dark skin. "I based her likeness on the one I consider my soul mate. He was my best friend. But we were young; we partied a lot. We made bad choices we very much regret now. I heard he has a family now—two daughters, my friend Greg said—but I never got to meet them. I guess I'm just too ashamed to, if they knew the things we did. But I do hope to meet them one day."

Pepper bites her lower lip. I look away, but I can feel her eyes on me. Rom's talking about Daddy, I'm sure of it. Ate Nadine's Ninong Greg did say they were friends in the old days. They were party people, he said. And Rom just confirmed it.

The model *is* based on Dad.

The sick feeling in my stomach is getting worse, and I feel like throwing up in a minute.

Pepper takes my hand, and her touch gives me the assurance I need.

I can't back out now. I need to ask the question.

Taking a deep breath, I exhale slowly and meet the man's gaze. "Is that man you're referring to Christopher Dulce?"

"Yes!" Rom's jaw drops. "How did you know?"

Ate Nadine puts an arm around my shoulders and says, "We're his daughters."

CHAPTER SEVENTEEN
Life Will Go On

AWKWARD.

Awkward is the only way I can describe the silence between us. Like, the awkwardest awkward silence ever. Even Pepper is at a loss for words.

Rom shifts his feet and clears his throat. Still, his voice comes out like a croak. "How is Christopher?"

I look up at my sister. Call me a coward, but I'm not the one breaking the ice.

"Oh man." Rom groans. "I'm so sorry. You might think I'm terrible for saying all those things to you."

"No, it's okay. We get it." Ate Nadine gives him a reassuring smile. "Our parents are separated. He lives in Pililla now."

"Yes. He's in Pililla *with his boyfriend*." Pepper throws me a knowing look, then stares Rom in the eye. "We love Wendell. You're not trying to be Tito Christopher's other boyfriend, are you?"

Kuya Jepoy coughs, trying to hide his laugh but failing spectacularly.

"No, no. No. Definitely not," says Rom. He holds up his hands and lets out a nervous chuckle. "It's just that . . . Your lola Cordia was religious and conservative. I thought you didn't know—"

"That our dad dates men and women?" Well, I can't blame him for thinking that way. I read online that Dad's identity is something not everyone will understand. "I think we're lucky. Ate and I have three dads!"

"Three? Ah. Ginnette has a boyfriend too." Rom smiles. "I agree. You have a lovely family."

"Yeah. Mom and Tito Ed have been together for three years now. Wendell and Dad, five years." Ate Nadine peers at Rom. "How long have you known our father?"

"Since forever." Rom looks wistfully at the *Soul Mates* painting. "We met in the summer before college. Tita Cordia didn't want him staying at a dorm while he studied in Pignatelli. So she and your grandpa bought a house in Quezon City. They went home to Pililla during the weekends and holidays. I lived on the same street with my mother."

"Their family lives in that house in Quezon City." Pepper tilts her head. "I'm at Sab's, like, every day. How come we never see you around?"

Rom points his thumb to the direction of the poster with his name on it. "I moved to New York twenty-four years ago. The summer before my senior year in college, if I remember right."

I do a quick calculation in my head. Mom said that she and Dad began dating in their last year of college—just after Romeo Gamelon left.

A frown creases my forehead. I hope Dad didn't date Mom just because he was sad about Rom leaving. "You still talked to Dad even after he was married?"

"Yes, but not as much. We lost touch in about a year or two. I wish I was there for him when he—" Rom's eyes flicker to the *Downward Spiral* photo. "When he wasn't well."

"It's okay. You can say it." I try not to roll my eyes. What is it with adults and avoiding the proper word for stuff? "Dad had depression."

Rom raises an eyebrow, and Ate Nadine shakes her head. If they're sharing a secret, I want in on it. I open my mouth to speak, but my sister is faster.

"We still have a few minutes left before the museum closes," she says, glancing at her watch. I don't get it. Her ninong said this man has the answers she seeks, and yet she's not asking him anything. Not the important questions anyway. "Why don't you show us around? I'm sure the girls have some questions."

"I have a question!" Pepper waves her hand in the air. But the intense look she gives Romeo Gamelon is far from comical. "Did you kill the dog?"

"Huh?"

"That one. In the first frame." I point to the photo near the door. "*Life Will Go On.*"

"Ah!" Rom's expression clears. "No, of course not. The dog is actually just sleeping. Come, look closer."

We follow the artist across the gallery. When I see the dog this time, I don't feel horrified anymore.

"See?" Rom says. "Just sleeping."

True, the dog isn't dead. He just looks dead. Rom tells us that the dog, named Hot Dog (really?) belonged to the street vendor selling hot dogs nearby (ugh, it's not even funny). Hot Dog liked sleeping near the gutter because it's cooler there. He was perfectly safe.

Rom gives us a personalized tour of his gallery, telling us the story behind each photograph. I'm not sure most of them are entirely true. Sometimes, he'll be enthusiastically discussing something about substance abuse, then he'll look at Ate Nadine and stop mid-sentence. It's almost as if he's asking for her permission.

He does, however, have a lot to say about how the government and media are dealing with the substance abuse problem. "The media should also be promoting health services for substance abuse, but the government itself should put more money into those projects instead of unlawful arrests that almost always end badly."

Rom also explains how his pictures follow a certain theme. "Things aren't always what they seem, see? You mustn't be so quick to judge. Anybody, rich or poor, can suffer from substance abuse. And sometimes, people suffering from it are the ones you least expect."

I notice he skips *Soul Mates*, which turns out to be the only photograph that had a female model who reminds me of Dad.

It seems to me that my question has already been answered, but I just don't know what I'm supposed to be asking. My initial question of "Do you know what happened between Ate Nadine and Dad?" isn't the right one to ask. After all, Ate Nadine also just met Rom today. There's something more to this story, but I can't pinpoint what it is exactly.

Well, an idea is forming in my head. But it just seems so terrible, even my wild imagination refuses to acknowledge it.

If Rom's art is based on real life, it can only mean that Dad is hiding something. And that something is bad, very bad.

CHAPTER EIGHTEEN
Chicken Sopas

THREE HOURS.

It took us three hours to get home and then we spent another thirty minutes dropping Pepper off and going back to Quezon City. My legs collapse under me, and I fall back on the couch. Ate Nadine dumps her bag on the table and slumps on the seat beside me.

"That bad, eh?" Tito Ed appears behind us. He rubs his hands down the front of his apron. "You must be hungry. Come join me and Lawin in the kitchen. I made chicken sopas."

I'm exhausted. I just want to close my eyes and sleep right here on the couch, but it's hard to say no to Tito Ed's chicken sopas.

"Hmm," Ate Nadine murmurs as she swallows a spoonful of the hot soup. "That's amazing."

And it certainly is. The chicken soup with milk, macaroni, and vegetables warms me up and soothes my tired bones. It's the best comfort food ever, the kind of food you eat when you're sick or feeling awful.

But for some reason, the sopas' comfort magic isn't working for me tonight. My body is warm and has everything it needs to relax, but this nagging feeling I got from the exhibit just won't leave me. It has followed me home all the way from Makati City like a restless ghost bent on making my life miserable.

"You should have called me," Tito Ed says as my sister finishes telling him about our train misadventures for the day. "I could have had someone pick you up at the MRT station."

"What? And waste taxpayers' money?" Ate Nadine rolls her eyes. "They're paying you to serve and protect the Filipino people, not just Sab and me."

Tito Ed chuckles. "That's true."

They then proceed to have a boring discussion about the traffic situation in Metro Manila. I stifle a yawn and tune them out.

I stir my sopas. Macaroni noodles and tiny bits of celery, carrots, and onion swirl as they're dragged into the tunnel of milky soup. It's kind of like Romeo Gamelon's photo of the staircase, *The Downward Spiral*.

There are a lot of things bugging me about that photo exhibit. For one, it had a photo with a model who looks remarkably like Dad—like his twin, even. Then, there's the family scene with the birthday boy sadly waiting for someone while his anxious mother keeps staring at the clock. It's just way too familiar.

I splash my soup and a carrot tidbit falls on my arm. I flick it off and rub the spot clean with my thumb. I remember touching a similar spot on Dad's arm—Dad's arm full of tiny dot scars. "Ants like to bite me," he said. "Don't tell Mom. She doesn't like ants."

It had been our little secret, but I think Mom knew.

"You're very quiet tonight, Sab," remarks Tito Ed. His mention of my name jolts me back to the present. "Are you all right?"

"I'm just tired," I say. It's true. I *am* tired. But maybe not in the way he thinks.

Ate Nadine throws me an odd look. I think she'll say

something, but she doesn't. She simply returns to her discussion with Tito Ed about the politics behind the lack of proper maintenance of the MRT. I let my mind wander back to Romeo Gamelon's gallery.

Recovery. Rom explained that's basically what his exhibit was about. He didn't mention it, but it was on the gallery description and pretty obvious in the art: It wasn't just about any recovery. It was about recovery from substance abuse.

Substance. I've encountered that exact word online. If I remember right, it was on the same website that told me what the purple-and-pink building in Pasig is for. The place wasn't just for people who have mental illness. It was also a rehabilitation center for patients recovering from alcoholism and drug addiction.

I let the vegetable pieces fall from my spoon and into the soup.

"Is there something wrong with your soup, Sab?" Tito Ed asks, his eyes on the utensil in my hand.

Get a grip, Sab.

"It's fine." I take a mouthful of my sopas, giving him a small smile. I can feel Ate Nadine's eyes on me, but I avoid her gaze.

"You can just finish that tomorrow, if you want." There's a loud screech as Tito Ed stands and pushes his chair away from the table. He clears the table, taking his and Ate Nadine's empty bowls to the sink. He lets the water run for a bit, then turns off the tap. "I'll wash these tomorrow. Don't tell your mom we left dirty dishes overnight."

A secret. It's another secret Mom shouldn't know about.

Ate Nadine cleans the table as Tito Ed transfers the leftover sopas to an empty plastic container. I always like seeing Tito Ed when he's not in his blue police uniform, wearing just a plain shirt and running shorts.

Tito Ed clears his throat. "Well, I better head to bed. There's more sopas in the container. Get some if you want. Just don't forget to put it in the fridge when the soup cools—"

"We got this, Tito Ed." My sister gets up from the table and walks to my side. Tito Ed bids us good night, but it's only Ate Nadine who responds.

I continue to stare at my bowl, and Ate Nadine comes to sit next to me.

"Listen, Sab. About the exhibit . . ."

I dip my spoon back into the sopas and stir it again. Around and around, the vegetables and chicken bits spin like a washing machine cycle, or debris trapped in a tornado destroying every-thing in its wake.

"I now realize it might not have been a good idea to let you go in once I saw what the show was about," my sister contin-ues. "But we were there already, and I thought it could help prepare you for the truth . . . the truth about Dad."

It's as if somebody turns on a switch, and a slide show begins to flash in my head.

The forgotten birthdays.

The broken promises.

The downward spiral with no means of escape.

"No." My heart pounds so fast, I almost have trouble speak-ing. "Dad couldn't be . . . Those three years we visited him in Pasig . . . No one bothered to tell me. Mom said . . . You *all* said he had a medical condition!"

I should have known better.

The truth, or what I thought was the truth. The secrets. The lies.

They're all falling into place, one by one.

"Dad wasn't in that center for depression." I put down the spoon, finally meeting my sister's gaze. "He was there for something else."

It's a statement, not a question. Still, I want it to be wrong. I want Ate Nadine to tell me I'm mistaken.

I clench my fist as a tear rolls down my cheek. Ate Nadine tucks a wet strand of hair behind my ear, gently cupping my cheek.

"I'm so sorry, Sab," she says. "Dad *was* in rehab for his drug addiction. He is a recovering addict."

CHAPTER NINETEEN
Lies, Lies, and More Lies

FRIDAY

TWO DAYS. THAT'S ALL I have left, if the Butterfly's warning is real. After last night? How can I trust anything Dad told me? The omen of the black butterfly was probably just a story he came up with. I should feel relieved, but I'm too upset.

It's almost lunch already, but I'm still lying in bed. My blinds are shut tight. It's as if night has come.

Fairy lights dangling between the bedposts of my headboard twinkle like stars in the dark. My phone belts out the *DuckTales* theme song for what seems like the fiftieth time.

Pepper has been calling and texting all morning, but I've been ignoring her. I ignore this call too.

I can't deal right now, and I just want to be alone.

KREEEN! The door creaks open. Somebody turns off the fairy lights and switches on the main ceiling lamp.

"Get up." It's Ate Nadine. "Come down to the study. Mom's online. She wants to talk to you."

I rub my eyes at the sudden brightness. It takes a few seconds for the spots in my vision to clear.

"*Now*, Sab."

Sighing, I do as my sister says. It's just not worth arguing anymore.

Nothing is worth it anymore.

I see Mom's face as soon as I sit on the office chair. Her face is perfectly made up, but a few strands of black hair have escaped her tight bun. Behind her is a red curtain. I'm guessing she's video calling in between sessions.

"Hi, sweetie. I love your new haircut!" she exclaims. It's only been a week, but how I miss that smile. "How's Pepper? Where's Lawin?"

Mom's trying to lighten the mood, but it's not working.

"Pepper's at her house." I left my phone upstairs, so I wouldn't know if Pepper called again. She probably hasn't and has moved on. It's not like she's going to keep on calling me forever. It's not okay, but I understand. After all, who wants a friend with an ex-addict dad? "Lawin's in the yard with Ate. He's playing in the mud and looking for bugs."

"Eww." Mom makes a face. "Be sure to give him a bath before you let him in the house."

I shrug. With the way things are going, Lawin should do whatever he wants. I'm not telling him off for having fun.

"How are you, sweetheart?"

Awful. Hurt. Betrayed. "I'm fine."

Mom bites her lower lip, the same way Ate Nadine does. "Tito Ed told me about last night."

"Okay." Of course he would. Tito Ed tells her *everything*. I wish they did the same with me.

"Do you want to talk about it?

"No."

Mom touches the computer screen. "I wish I could be there and give you a hug."

"Me too."

"Sabrina." Mom sighs. "I told you. I couldn't say no to the organizers. This is a once-in-a-lifetime opportunity—"

"I know, Mom."

Mom is an urban planner who works for a private firm but gives free consultations for the government whenever she has time. It's one of the reasons why she and Tito Ed are so great together—they have the similar goal of wanting to make the lives of Filipinos better. But this same goal is costing the time she could have spent with me.

I feel bad being such a brat like this, but give me some credit. A supernatural (and probably fictional) insect told me I'm dying. I found out my own father used to do drugs, and everyone kept it a secret from me. And I'm turning eleven, and Mom is too busy trying to fix Metro Manila's traffic problems to celebrate with me. This week is terrible. So yeah. I think I deserve to be bratty just for a bit.

"What's on your mind, sweetheart? You can ask me anything. I'd like to explain—"

I avert my eyes. They fall on the window beside me, the one with the family picture sitting on the windowsill. It overlooks the shed in the garden. It used to be Dad's studio, where he spent days (sometimes even weeks) working on a piece.

"How long has Dad been using drugs?"

On-screen, Mom's gaze flickers on the mantel. She sighs. "When we were still in college, I was sure he was using. He skipped a semester for rehab and got well from it. You were two when I had a feeling he was using again. But I wasn't sure," says Mom. "Listen, sweetheart, addiction is a disease."

"I know, I know." It takes every bit of my willpower not to roll my eyes. The office chair creaks as I lean on the backrest. It holds the lingering scent of Ate Nadine's body spray of strawberries and cream. "Tito Ed told me."

"You must understand this, baby. Just bear with me for a bit." Mom's face grows closer to my screen. "Your asthma. What do you do when your chest feels tight and you feel lightheaded because you can't breathe?"

"I take my inhaler. What does that have to do with—"

"You need your medicine to keep it at bay," Mom says with a nod. "But remember what the doctor said? One day, you might not need your inhaler anymore. Still, the asthma will always be part of you, and you'll need to keep constant vigilance so it won't come back."

As if on cue, my chest begins to tighten. I take a deep breath and let air out slowly to keep my pulse at a normal rate.

"Dad's disease is like your asthma," Mom continues. "Lola Cordia got him help before you and Nadine were born. He was fine, then he got sick with it once more. The people at the medical facility helped him get well. He's been okay. He's doing everything he can to stay okay, because he loves us and doesn't want his addiction to cause him to make bad choices again."

A terrible realization punches me in the gut. "Was it because of me?"

"Sweetheart. Sabrina. Sab. Look at me." Mom moves even closer to the screen. "It's *not* your fault. It's never your fault."

Tears well up in my eyes. What if Mom's wrong? There must have been something I missed, something I could have done. Something I did.

"Sab, it's got nothing to do with what you did or didn't do," Mom insists, shaking her head. There's so much urgency in her voice, I lean back on the office chair to move away. "We all have things we want so much that we find it hard to say no to them. Chocolate is bad for my blood sugar, but I still love it. There are times I want it so much, I make the wrong choice and indulge myself even if I know it's bad for me. Dad dealt with something similar. He knew it was bad for him, but he picked the wrong choice and hurt us."

"That's the reason why you left him, isn't it, Mommy?"

Mom looks down at her keyboard. Even without words, her silence screams yes.

My hands shake. My chest tightens. "How come you never told me?"

"I'm so sorry, sweetheart. I thought it would protect you. This isn't how I wanted you to find out—"

I blink furiously to stop the tears from falling. "I wish you were here, Mommy."

"Me too." Mom kisses the tips of her index and middle fingers and places them on the screen.

I touch the screen where Mom's fingers are. "When are you coming back?"

"The conference will be over later in the afternoon, but there's a tour this weekend. They'll show Singapore urban planning in action, which I think will be very helpful for my personal project. So if all goes well, I'll be in Manila by Monday. It'll still be your birthday on the other side of the world. We'll celebrate again, okay? Anything you want."

I'm not sure if she's trying to convince herself, or me.

"Listen, sweetie." Mom lets out a long sigh. "I'm going to try my best to be home as soon as I can. I'll bring you salted egg potato chips and lots and lots of chocolate. And, Sab?"

"Hmm?"

"Can you please tell Ate to go online when she's done making lunch? I'd like to talk to her."

I nod.

"Thanks, sweetie. Love you!"

We hang up, the computer chiming as I shut it down. Soon, I see nothing but a black screen.

I lay my head on the desk and let the tears flow.

CHAPTER TWENTY
Smelly Vampire Girl

THE SIZZLING SOUNDS OF KWEK-KWEK are making my tummy grumble, but my heart doesn't want food. My heart wants nothing but to be alone.

Yes, I'm being overly dramatic. But I've gotten to a point where I feel like I can't trust anyone, you know?

Like today, for example.

I don't know what Mom and Ate Nadine talked about. But the moment we finished eating lunch, Ate Nadine dragged me to the shower to get cleaned up and ready. I was perfectly content in my dirty pajamas with Lawin and a huge bag of cheese balls on my bed all day. But no. Ate Nadine had to ruin my plans.

"You're coming with me out in the sun, Smelly Vampire Girl," she demanded. My sister practically carried me to her car. But the worst part? "We're picking up Pepper."

So here I am, back in the alley near Ate Nadine's school. Alone on a bench with the friend who will soon un-friend me once she gets too full to eat kwek-kwek. My sister is across the alley from us, browsing for a laptop cover. Every now and then, she'll sneak a peek at us.

Ate Nadine wanted me to tell Pepper about Dad, because Pepper's my best friend.

My best friend *for now*, at least. I doubt she'll still want to be once she finds out.

Thing is, I can sit here all day with my mouth shut and my hair smelling like fried quail eggs, but I'm not saying a word. I'm done with people lying to me and telling me what to do. All week, I've believed my fate is tied to the Butterfly of Death. But, as it turns out, the so-called supernatural insect was likely just a figment of my father's imagination.

None of it was real, and I was a fool to believe it.

I was a fool to believe in Dad, *period*.

"Aren't you going to ask me what's wrong?" The words surprise me as they come out of my mouth.

"Do you want me to?" Pepper crushes and tosses her empty kwek-kwek cup. It lands squarely inside the black trash bag hanging on the vendor's cart beside her.

"Are you serious?" My eyes narrow. Pepper's not into discussing emotions, but come on. "Aren't you even at least curious?"

"I am. But you didn't answer any of my calls or texts or chat messages, so I figure you don't want to tell me."

"Why did you come, then?"

"Your sister called me," she explains. "It's hard to say no when Ate Nadine demands for me to get ready so she can pick me up."

"Well, you didn't have to come." All along I thought she was concerned about me. I guess I'm wrong. Again.

"Duh. Of course I'd go." Pepper twists a lock of brown hair around her finger. She sighs. "Okay, fine. I'll bite. Why are you ignoring me, Sab? What did I do?"

"I'm not—" I let out a sigh. There's no point in prolonging this any further. If she wants to stop being my friend after this, then it's better to get it over with. "My dad is a recovering drug addict."

Pepper lets go of her hair. She turns to look at me, her blue eyes meeting my brown ones. "Yeah, I figured."

"You did?" *Okay.* That was unexpected.

"My papa was a missionary, remember? Part of his mission was to volunteer at rehab facilities," Pepper says, waving her hand dismissively. "Not the same one your grandma sent your dad to—the purple-and-pink building is for people who can afford it. Papa worked at government-run centers."

The knot in my stomach begins to unwind. "When did you know?"

"Our first homeroom assignment together, when we had to write about our families."

I raise an eyebrow.

"I wasn't sure until we met Romeo Gamelon. He said they used to party a lot . . . Parties are usually where people get their drugs. And that gallery was kind of a dead giveaway." Pepper holds on to the edge of the bench, steadying herself. It really is hard to keep balance on the thin planks turned makeshift bench. "You'll be surprised how common your story is. Your mama left your papa after he did something to you and Ate Nadine, didn't she?"

"Yeah." I was only four when it happened, but I remember the day. Ate Nadine was almost eleven, like me now. Dad was supposed to take us to the mall, but he made this sudden turn and parked near an alley similar to this one. He left Ate and me at a bakery, promising he wouldn't be long.

Dad didn't return until it was very dark. Mom and Lola Cordia were already there with cops and an ambulance. I can't forget how Dad looked—his eyes were dilated, his skin flushed, and he was as pale as a ghost. Lola Cordia took us to a nearby restaurant to eat dinner. Mom joined us soon after. She tried to hide it, but it was obvious—she'd been crying.

We didn't see Dad for six months, until we visited him in the facility at Pasig. We saw him every few months or so, but eventually, he faded from our lives. Dad moved to Pililla, while we stayed in Quezon City. We saw him sometimes, but our visits were mostly because of Lola Cordia. Dad met Wendell, and Mom met Tito Ed. Then Lola Cordia died last year, and we haven't seen him since. It's like Lola Cordia was the only one keeping the family together. But she's gone, and this is where we're at now.

Pepper touches my hand. She doesn't say anything. Most people would probably say, "I'm sorry," like it's their fault or something, when it's obviously not. Just being with me, just being my friend—I appreciate it more.

I turn to face Pepper on the bench. "I thought you'd stop being my friend if you found out."

"Seriously?" Pepper's blue eyes widen. Then she snorts. "Geez, Sab. I'm your *best* friend. There's nothing for you to be ashamed of. I won't deserve to even call you a 'friend-friend' if I stop being friends with you because of that."

"Really?"

"Really." My friend gives me a firm nod. "You can talk to me about it whenever you want."

"Thank you." Before Pepper can talk again, I rush in to hug her. "You are the *bestest* best friend ever."

Pepper stiffens. She pats my back and eventually hugs me in return.

"This is weird," Pepper mumbles, her breath warm on my ear. "So weird."

"It's not." I loosen my grip but keep my arms around her. It's not often I get to hug Pepper. She's allergic to affection.

"You can let go now. People are looking at us weird."

"Oh." I let go and try to laugh, but all that comes out is a sound that's a cross between laughing and crying. It's such a relief to know I'm not losing my friend.

"Sab!" Pepper groans. "Don't cry. Or I'm going to cry."

"I'm not crying," I say, but sniff and wipe away my tears with the back of my hand. As my vision clears, it lands on Ate

Nadine. She's still across the alley, keeping a respectful distance, smiling at us. Kuya Jepoy joins her. Together, they walk to where we are.

Kuya Jepoy gets down on his knees so we're at eye level. He puts his hands on my shoulders. "Can I also get a hug?"

I throw my arms around him. Kuya Jepoy smells like cinnamon, different from Ate Nadine, but somehow, comfortingly familiar. He hugs me back.

"It's okay, kiddo. We're here for you. Remember that," he says. Kuya Jepoy strokes my hair. "You're never alone."

Ate Nadine grins at me. "How about we go shopping now, Smelly Vampire Girl?"

"I'm not smelly." I pout, but the corners of my mouth betray me. They're curling up in a smile. "Can I buy new oil pastels at the strip mall, Ate? The ones they sell here are so hard and brittle—"

"PULIS! PULIS!" a man in the alley shouts, warning about the police.

My chest tightens as my heart falls to my stomach. I try not to overreact like I did the last time, so I keep my panic at bay.

"You must go, children." To my surprise, it's the kwek-kwek vendor who speaks. He looks at Kuya Jepoy. "Bring them to your workplace. You'll be safe there."

Oh, it's for real this time. I grab the inhaler from my pocket and take a puff. "Why? What's going on?"

"Raid," the vendor says grimly. "There's an article in the *Manila Daily Journal* this morning. About some punk selling drugs to college kids. They're probably looking for—"

Ate Nadine gasps. "What do you mean, an article?" She turns to me. "I didn't know it was coming out today. My boss texted me something this morning about 'going forward,' but it didn't occur to me she meant 'going forward with publishing.' I was so worried about you and—"

Gunshots erupt in the alley, echoing in the deafening silence that follows.

Ate Nadine grabs me by the scruff of my shirt, pulling me on the ground with her. Kuya Jepoy does the same for Pepper.

"Get those kids out of here, Jepoy!" the kwek-kwek vendor says as he holds on to his cart. His pan of bubbling oil threatens to spill as people stampede out of the alley.

He doesn't have to tell us twice. We leap up and run as fast as our feet can carry us.

CHAPTER TWENTY-ONE
Operation Tokhang

WE RUN THROUGH THE ALLEY, zigzagging between people while avoiding merchandise strewn all over the ground. I feel lightheaded, and I'm finding it harder and harder to breathe.

I slow down, trying to catch my breath.

"We're almost there, Sab." Ate Nadine tugs my hand. "Just hold on for a bit longer."

I can't speak, so I nod and take another deep breath.

We pass by the ice cream parlor as Kuya Jepoy leads us out of the alley, where we turn left and run a bit more. Three stores down, he stops at an internet café and opens the door.

Chimes tinkle as we enter, and cold, air-conditioned air blasts my face. I bend over, holding my side. My head nearly hits the tower of box-type computer monitors piled high near the entrance.

"Careful," Kuya Jepoy warns. "Sorry about the mess. My boss is replacing the old box monitors with the newer, flat ones."

Pepper and Ate Nadine pull me upright, and one of them shoves the blue medicine canister in my hand.

"Take a puff again," Ate Nadine orders. I do as I'm told. My heart is still racing, but my breathing is better now. I don't feel like I'm drowning anymore.

"Thanks, Ate."

"Oh, wow." Pepper collapses in the computer chair nearest her. I do the same. "That was intense."

Ate Nadine purses her lips, but she doesn't reply.

"Jepoy, what happened?" We look up and find a middle-aged woman behind the counter at the far end of the internet café. Her hair is as short as mine. If not for her voice, I would have mistaken her for a man.

"It was a Tokhang, boss," Kuya Jepoy says. He hurries to the woman's side, helping her onto a chair. "Someone must have gotten in the way."

"Who?"

"We don't know." Kuya Jepoy shrugs.

I feel my heart drop to my stomach. Oh no. Did somebody actually *die*?

Ate Nadine's frown deepens. She walks past the rows of computers to the counter where the woman is standing. There's a small fridge beside the cashier.

"Three bottles of mineral water, please." Ate Nadine pays the woman, and Kuya Jepoy hands Pepper and me a bottle each. We drink them down as though we've been stuck in the desert for days.

Pepper lets out a loud burp when she's done. "What's 'Tokhang'?"

My sister, Kuya Jepoy, and the woman exchange grim, knowing looks.

"Operation Tokhang. It's a police operation named after a combination of Visayan words. *Tuktok*, which means 'to knock.' And *hangyo*, which means 'to plead or persuade.'" Ate Nadine rubs her temples as she explains. "The idea is that police will visit suspected drug users and pushers and try to convince them to stop their illegal activities and offer rehabilitation and other livelihood programs."

"That doesn't sound so bad." Pepper tilts her head.

I run my hand through my short hair. Ate Nadine's

explanation reminds me of the man who gave me this cut. "The stylist said there's nothing to worry about if you're not doing or selling drugs."

"In essence, yes. There are some places where it works as it should," Ate Nadine says. "But there are trigger-happy cops who abuse their power, and corrupt officials who use it for their own gain. So people die."

I've heard Tito Ed mention having police operations against the drug trade, but I never knew what it's called. I didn't think it involved people dying either. After all, Tito Ed himself used to be a correctional facility officer, focusing particularly on those who needed help from drug use. I can't imagine him shooting somebody just because they're suspected of doing illegal activities. I can't imagine him hurting anyone, period.

But after the past week? I don't know. There are so many things I've been so wrong about, things I've thought to be one thing but turn out to be another.

Just look at my dad. All along I thought he was this kind, fun, and doting father I grew up with. The father who shared with me his great love for art. Turns out, all along everyone was lying to me.

"Ate, the stylist said bad cops believe the president—that he wants all drug people dead . . ." A horrible thought enters my mind. "Do those people include Daddy?"

Ate Nadine and Kuya Jepoy exchange glances.

"Sab, Pepper." Ate Nadine pats the computer chair beside her. "Come sit beside me."

We do as my sister asks. Pepper twirls a lock of hair around her finger, but she doesn't say anything. I don't either. We simply sit on our computer chairs and stare at the blank screens in front of us in silence.

"Listen to me, girls." Ate Nadine clears her throat. She pauses, taking a gulp of her bottled water. "We're very, very fortunate. We may not be like those rich families who can afford mansions and sports cars, but we get by better than most Filipinos. Dad is okay now because Lola Cordia had the money to pay for his rehabilitation. The majority of Filipinos wouldn't be able to afford that, and they rely on the government to help them recover.

"So to answer your question, yes, the people arrested in these raids are no different than Dad, except that they have less money. Had Dad been in their same place, he probably would have been arrested too, or worse. And if Dad ever did get arrested, he'd get off easy because he can afford treatment and the help of a lawyer."

"That's unfair." Pepper frowns. "Why do people get special treatment just because they have more money? No offense."

"None taken. It's called 'privilege.'" Ate Nadine gives Pepper a smile. "It's just like when the security guard let you take the 'better' train car because he thinks your being white makes you deserve it."

Pepper pouts. "It's not my fault I look like this."

"That's true, of course. But this privilege is given to you without question, willingly, because of our culture steeped in the scars of a colonized past. It's up to you what to make of it. You can either recognize and understand your privilege so you can make our society better, or you don't and let things stay the same."

"Didn't Daddy take advantage of his privilege, Ate?" I ask, sneaking a glance at Kuya Jepoy, who's been hanging back to give us privacy. He's trying to turn his life around. But Kuya Jepoy can't afford a college education, nor can he accept a scholarship, because he needs to work and feed his lola and five sisters.

Dad threw away an entire semester because of his addiction.

He wasted the very opportunity many people would love to have. He did something illegal and escaped the consequences because he had money.

I'm not angry (seriously). Well, maybe a little. Fine. *I am.*

"He did, kiddo." To my surprise and Ate Nadine's, it's Kuya Jepoy who answers. He gives me a kind smile. "You remember when I told you about my uncle going to prison?"

I nod. Pepper shakes her head, but I mouth, "I'll tell you later."

"He was caught by the police selling drugs," Kuya Jepoy continues. "He knew it was wrong. And yet, he still made the choice to do it. Maybe he felt like it was the only way to make money, or he didn't consider the danger of it. But just because someone messes up doesn't automatically mean they're a bad person." Kuya Jepoy glances at Ate Nadine. My sister avoids his gaze. "Good people can make bad choices too."

Mom said the same thing, that Dad made the wrong choices. Maybe they're right. Dad wouldn't have willingly put himself in danger like that if his mind had been well. I should be glad he didn't die.

The thought of Daddy lying in the alley with all those cops and panicking people— No, I'm not thinking about it.

"Is there a computer I can use?" I clear my throat, hoping to rid myself of the lump threatening to make me cry. Now's not the time to cry about Dad.

"There's one in the corner. I'll show you," Kuya Jepoy says before the shop owner can answer. Ate Nadine tries to protest as Pepper stands to join me, but Kuya Jepoy shakes his head. He leads me to the back of the room, to the far corner, away from everyone. "I figured you'd want to be alone."

"Thanks." I give him a watery smile. "Am I that obvious?"

Kuya Jepoy reaches out to ruffle my hair. "You're like Nadine in a lot of ways—she's very sensitive." He chuckles as he sets up the computer for me. "She is. She just doesn't like showing it. But that doesn't mean she doesn't care."

I pull up the web browser when Kuya Jepoy leaves to join Ate Nadine and Pepper at the front of the internet café. Typing in the address of the black Butterfly website (I know it by heart), I press Enter.

I may not be convinced it's real anymore, but I feel like I need to see it. It's just easier to worry about the Butterfly taking me instead of worrying about my dad.

A familiar website appears, where an animated image of a

giant, black-as-night butterfly loads in the middle. It flaps its wings slowly as more of the animation file downloads.

ONE HUNDRED PERCENT, says the indicator. The file is fully downloaded.

But the flapping doesn't slow down.

The animated butterfly flaps faster and faster. It flaps so fast, the wings resemble nothing but a black blur.

I shut my eyes to clear the vision away. I'm tired, that's all. I'm seeing odd things.

When I open my eyes, the black blur is gone.

Perched on the flat screen, right on the spot where the image was . . . is a giant black butterfly.

My head spins as my heart drops to my stomach once again. Still, I muster the courage to reach out and touch it. I jump— the Butterfly's wings are soft and velvety, but cold as ice.

It's real, all right. *Very* real.

I stare at the Butterfly as it flaps its wings twice, then launches from the monitor. It flies up the ceiling, fading in the florescent light. "Ate—"

The door chimes tinkle as somebody enters the internet café.

"POLICE! Taas ang kamay!"

From the safety of my corner, I see the internet café owner, Kuya Jepoy, Pepper, and my sister raise their hands in the air as two cops walk inside. I do the same, and one of the officers sees me. He beckons me to come to the front with my sister and friends. I willingly follow.

"Put your hands down," says his partner. He points at Kuya Jepoy. "Except for you."

"What? No." I spread my arms wide in front of Kuya Jepoy. "He didn't do anything."

The officer scowls at Ate Nadine. "Tell the girl to get out of the way or she's coming with us to the precinct."

"It's okay, Sab." Kuya Jepoy gives me a sad smile as the cops cuff him. "I'll be fine. They're just going to ask me questions."

Didn't they just say bad cops will only treat people well if they have money? "But—"

"Sab, don't." Ate Nadine grips my shoulders. "I'll ask Tito Ed to handle this."

The door chimes tinkle once again, and Kuya Jepoy leaves with the mean cops.

I think I'm going to throw up. They're taking my friend like he's a criminal.

CHAPTER TWENTY-TWO
Faith and Fate

SATURDAY

I'M ON THE BACK PORCH alone, watching Lawin dunk his head in a basin of water in the garden. He then wags his tail. He repeats this ten times, before waddling to the pile of sliced cucumbers and cherry tomatoes in his food bowl on the grass.

It must be nice, being a duck. All you have to do is wake up, eat, swim, drink, and sleep. You don't have to worry about doomsday butterflies, allergy attacks, or getting your friend arrested.

Yes, the Butterfly is real after all. I saw it with my own eyes—again.

If Pepper were here, my day might have been happier and less boring. Today's the day Pepper has been waiting for—the day she becomes a junior bridesmaid instead of a flower girl. It's very important to her. Because today, her family will recognize she's not a little girl anymore.

Still, I wish Pepper were here with me.

It's selfish, I know, but you have to understand—tomorrow's my last day. I would have wanted to have Pepper by my side if I *do* die. I need my friend. Especially when another one is currently in jail for something he didn't do.

"Sab," Tito Ed calls, poking his head out of the glass sliding doors. "I won't be long. Your sister is here, if you need anything."

I nod but say nothing.

"Nadine—"

"We'll be okay." Ate Nadine joins me on the bench as Tito Ed leaves with a sigh.

All morning, Tito Ed has been trying to assure me that Kuya Jepoy's fine. That he's taken care of it. Still, I find it hard to believe him. I've heard what bad cops can do. How can I be sure he's not like them? Nothing he says will make me feel better unless I see for myself that Kuya Jepoy is unharmed.

"That duck and I don't always get along, but we need to get him a bigger pool. He can't even fit his big butt in that basin." Ate Nadine puts her legs up on the wooden table. She waves her hand an inch from my nose. "Yoo-hoo! Earth to Sab."

I push her hand away. "What?"

"Hey." Ate Nadine pats my hand. "Jepoy is fine. You need to trust Tito Ed."

"Do you?"

My sister looks me straight in the eye while giving my hand a squeeze. "With my life."

"I just don't understand!" I exclaim, pulling my hand away. "Why did the cops arrest Kuya Jepoy? He didn't do anything!"

"Listen, Sab." Ate Nadine takes me by the shoulders, forcing me to face her. "Not all cops are like Tito Ed. There are those who wouldn't even give Jepoy due process. Many people are framed and killed because some cops just want to impress the president. Or maybe the bad cops sold drugs themselves and just want to cover up their deed. Our justice system isn't the same as what you see on American TV shows. Corruption makes it hard for the majority of Filipinos to have a day in court."

"But—"

"But Tito Ed called the headquarters as soon as I told him what happened. He made sure Jepoy is treated well during their questioning."

"Will Kuya Jepoy be okay?"

"Yes, Sab. I'm sure of it." Ate Nadine's voice is so quiet I can barely hear her. "I know it's hard for you to trust after finding this out about Dad. Believe me, I do too. Still, you need to have a little faith that people will get better. Because eventually, they do. Sometimes it takes a day, a month, or a year. Or maybe even longer than that. Either way, life will find a way to make things right."

It's almost as if she's saying it not just for my benefit but for hers as well.

From the patio, Ate Nadine and I get a perfect view of Marikina Valley, all the way to the mountains of Antipolo. On our left, there's a river snaking under a bridge, where cars, trucks, and jeepneys pass through. Their headlights are like red-and-yellow fireflies at dusk. They glint as the sun leaves and the moon takes its place.

This is the same view we get at dusk every day. Yet, it's only recently I've grown to truly appreciate it. It's quite interesting, really, how the appearance of the Butterfly changed the way I see things in such a short period of time.

My fate isn't in the hands (or wings) of a butterfly, but in my own.

Maybe I'll die today or tomorrow. Maybe I won't. Either way, it's time for me to take my fate in my hands again.

"Ate, I know you don't like Daddy—I'm angry too—but I need answers. I'd still like to spend my birthday at the resort. If you don't want to take Pepper and me there, that's okay. We'll ask Tito Ed." My heart pounds so fast, I almost have trouble speaking. "But it would be great if you can come with us."

I feel my sister tense up, but she continues to stare at the valley.

"Ate?"

"I heard you," she says. Ate Nadine finally turns to look at me. "All right."

I'm not sure I heard her correctly. "What do you mean, 'All right'?"

"'All right' as in, I'll do it. We'll have your party at the resort."

My jaw drops. "Really?"

"Really."

"Thank you!" I squeal in delight, throwing my arms around Ate Nadine. I lay my head on her shoulder, and she sighs.

The mosquitos are starting to come out, but Ate Nadine doesn't seem to care. I don't either. It's as if we both want the moment to go on forever, just the two of us. No butterflies. No lies. No bad cops. No Kuya Jepoy. No Pepper. No Wendell, no Tito Ed, no Mom, and no Dad. Just me and my big sister.

"Ahem."

We look behind us and find our mother standing on the patio. She wears a sweater too warm for the Philippine weather but which must have kept her from getting cold on the flight from Singapore to Manila. Mom's smile is as big as the moon above us. "What's going on here?"

"Mommy, you're home!"

CHAPTER TWENTY-THREE
The Gift of Change

SUNDAY

I'M ELEVEN TODAY. FUNNY, I don't feel any different. I'm nervous, but that's got nothing to do with me turning a year older.

It's a good thing Mom had us prepare everything last night. I think she felt guilty for almost missing my birthday. Or maybe she felt bad I found out about Dad's addiction. Or maybe our video call made her worry about me. But whatever, my mom's home! Mom arranged everything with Wendell as soon as I told her about wanting to celebrate my eleventh at Dad's resort.

"Wendell is an amazing party planner," she said. "He'll pull it off."

True. Spur-of-the-moment celebrations were no match for Wendell's planning skills.

We were able to leave the house by six, with the sun shining bright, and head for the strip mall to buy some things Wendell needed. Pepper slept over since her parents are usually busy in the morning tending to their backyard farm and gazillion animals.

I've been iffy about seeing the strip mall and the alley beside it (my memories of those places are less than pleasant), but I'm not going to let anything ruin this day.

Mom and Tito Ed head for the coffee shop. Ate Nadine takes Pepper and me along with her to the waiting shed in front of the salon to meet "somebody."

"Hey, kiddo," says a familiar low and soothing male voice. It's Kuya Jepoy. He shaved the stubble on his chin, and his clothes are pressed and clean.

I feel the knot in my stomach untangle. Kuya Jepoy is free!

Pepper grins. "We were afraid you'd be sent to prison."

"Pepper!" I swear, my friend can be so tactless at times. But yes, I'm so glad he didn't go to prison.

"Just for a bit. The orange prison shirt doesn't suit me." Kuya Jepoy ruffles our hair at the same time. He smiles at Ate Nadine. "Your tito Ed came to the precinct just minutes after Nadine called him. They asked me questions, but they treated me well."

"That's good." My sister's right. I shouldn't have doubted Tito Ed. "Are you coming with us for my party in Pililla? You're going to love it there. We don't have a farm, but the resort has a nice pool and lots of trees and Lola Cordia's butterfly garden is really beautiful."

I'm rambling like Pepper, but I can't help myself. I'm just so excited.

To my surprise, Kuya Jepoy shakes his head. "I'm just here to wish you happy birthday and bid you all goodbye."

"You didn't tell me that. I thought you were coming with us." Ate Nadine's eyes narrow. There's an accusing tone in her voice. "Where are you going? "

Kuya Jepoy stares at his feet. "Home."

"Will you come back?" Pepper asks, tilting her head.

"Maybe next summer." Kuya Jepoy gives me a small smile. "I just need to be with my family for a bit. My lola was really worried when I called her in the province. She needs some help at the farm anyway, so it's all for the best."

"*Still,*" Ate Nadine insists, scowling. "You should have told me."

"I'm sorry, Nadine." Kuya Jepoy touches my sister's hair. It's not like what he does with mine though. He gently tucks a lock behind her ear. It's pretty romantic, actually. Well, that is, until he follows it up with, "I *was* in jail."

Pepper and I burst out laughing.

"You can kiss her so she'll stop hating on you," my friend snickers.

"Shut up, Pepper," Ate Nadine growls.

My sister's scowl fades away as Kuya Jepoy takes her hand. He stares at her as he brings it to his lips.

Pepper and I squeal.

"Oh, be quiet." If Ate Nadine were as white as Pepper, she'd be blushing red by now.

Kuya Jepoy clears his throat. "Well, I'm going to miss you two."

"If you don't email us, your life is going to be very boring." Pepper gives him a quick hug. "Keep in touch, Kuya Jepoy."

"Of course." Kuya Jepoy gives her a wink.

Pepper's cheeks turn crimson. Ha! I knew it.

"Sab." Kuya Jepoy takes off his bracelet. To my surprise, he hands it to me. "When we meet again, I hope I'll have enough money to give you a proper gift. So think of this as your temporary birthday present."

I examine the wooden bracelet. This is too much. I can't accept it. "Your uncle gave this to you."

"It's pretty," Pepper says from over my shoulder.

"I know, and it's yours now." Kuya Jepoy shows me the bead shaped like a butterfly. "The butterfly is a symbol of change. People can change, Sab. Like my uncle did. Like your dad did. They've done bad things, and they've suffered for it. But they're still family."

A lump forms in my throat, and my lower lip quivers.

"Do you like it?"

"I love it!" I throw my arms around Kuya Jepoy as I let my tears fall. "I'll never forget it—I'll never forget you."

CHAPTER TWENTY-FOUR
Travel Time Times Ninety-Nine

LOLA CORDIA'S RESORT IS IN Pililla, Rizal. My web search said it's around 55.5 kilometers from where we live, and around two hours and thirty minutes to travel by car. Ate Nadine always said my internal GPS navigation is worse than those cheap knockoffs sold near her college. But even someone who's "directionally challenged" like myself can figure out we're far from Metro Manila.

We climb farther into the mountains of Antipolo, all the way to Manila East Road. It's a long stretch of highway going through several small towns, connecting each province to the next. We'll pass by a populated area every now and then. Most of the time, however, we see dense clusters of trees or vast, open fields.

I usually find these "in-between" parts of the trip enjoyable. Now, I can't stop thinking about how the highway seems to be lacking guardrails in a lot of places. If Tito Ed's not careful, he can drive off into a rice paddy, hit a grazing carabao, or fall into a ditch. None of these scenarios can bode well for somebody who's under the threat of dying—namely, me.

We spent the next hour with alternating views—small homes, trees, or open fields. But as we cross the border to Dad's town, we find ourselves on the side of a mountain. Tito Ed turns off the air conditioner and lowers the windows so we can savor the fresh air. Ate Nadine is fast asleep, but Pepper hands Lawin to me to relish the view without a duck pulling on her hair.

Wind turbines dot the slope near the peak, overlooking Laguna de Bay. The water sparkles under the morning sun, with fish pens forming geometric patterns on its surface.

Seeing the lake has always been my favorite part of our trips to Pililla. Actually, I love everything about going to Pililla—except for my butt hurting from sitting in a car so long.

Before long, we're back to the plains. Rice paddies flank both sides of the road, stretching all the way to the mountain foothills. Coconut and wild banana trees dot the properties, with a nipa hut or two in between. These traditional houses of bamboo and dried grass stick out like sore thumbs in the fields.

We pass under a concrete archway welcoming us to the town of Pililla. Little by little, man-made structures replace the greenery. Tito Ed is driving under the speed limit, so it's hard to miss the single-story, concrete houses on the sides of the road. Some are complete and painted, but many are not. They stand in their rustic, unpaved, pile-of-hollow-blocks state.

We're almost there.

And that's when the car overheats, and Tito Ed has to pull over on the side of the highway.

"Ginnette, love, did you bring your one-liter bottle of water?" he asks, gripping the steering wheel tight.

"No." Even from the back of the car, I can picture Mom narrowing her eyes the way Ate Nadine does when she's annoyed. "You said you have it covered—"

BOOM!

Mom and Tito Ed curse at the same time as the car lurches forward. Ate Nadine holds on to Pepper and me. I tighten my grip on Lawin, keeping him from flying off.

"Edwin!" Mom cries. "Why didn't you watch where you were parking?"

Tito Ed goes out of the car, cursing some more as he examines the damage.

"Ladies, you need to get out of the car," he tells us. "The radiator overheated, so I'm going to get water from that nearby house. The blown tire—"

"I'll take care of it." Ate Nadine gets out and heads for the car trunk, where Tito Ed keeps his tools and the spare tire.

Pepper groans. "But I need to pee!"

I frown at my friend. I had warned Pepper about drinking too much coconut juice, but she wouldn't listen. Where is she going to pee now? We've already passed the gas station, and that's, like, five rice fields away. She's my best friend and everything, but no way can I walk that far so she can pee.

"I got this." Mom gets out of the car, waving her shawl. "Come, Pepper. I'll teach you how to pee on a tree. Stay with your sister, Sab."

Pepper turns bright pink. I giggle. Well, it's not my fault she wouldn't stop drinking.

"Try not to pee on a duwende, Pepper!" I can't resist calling as my friend follows Mom to a cluster of trees. I'm too far to see, but I know when she turned around, she's sticking her tongue out at me.

Dad used to tell me about the duwendes—or dwarfs—living on trees. These creatures of myth can bring good or bad luck, depending if they like you or not. I'm pretty sure peeing on one would put you in the category of "do not like."

"Pepper will be fine." Ate Nadine rolls the spare tire to the side of the blown one. "Duwendes like to live in big trees like balete, mango, or bamboo. Not banana ones."

I deposit Lawin into his traveling crate and follow Ate Nadine. "Do you think it'll take us long here?"

"No," she says. "Stay away from the highway. We're not in a gated subdivision anymore. Cars won't stop if they see you."

I squat in front of Ate Nadine, leaning on the metal guard-rail. She pushes the car jack beneath the car, pumping it to lift the vehicle. I feel bad watching her do all the work, but I really have no idea how to change a tire. "Ate, do you think this is a good idea? You know, seeing Dad again?"

Ate Nadine stops pumping the jack. She takes her time before answering. "Yes, I believe so. I didn't at first. But Jepoy—" My sister tucks a hair behind her ear, just like what Kuya Jepoy did for her. "He's right. *You're* right. We need to give Dad a chance, Sab."

"I'm scared, Ate. I'm not sure I like him anymore, and I feel bad thinking that way."

Ate Nadine opens her mouth to speak but decides against it. She drops the jack and gathers me in her arms instead. The comforting smell of strawberries and cream engulfs me.

I take a deep breath, letting the air out slowly.

"It's hard for me too, Sab. It's okay to feel that way." My sister kisses my forehead. Lola Cordia used to do that whenever I was mad at Dad. It always made me feel better, and it still does. My heart still aches, but not as much as before. "You don't have to forgive him *now*, but keep your heart open. I'll try to, too."

I spin the wooden beads on my new bracelet and see the butterfly—the symbol of change. Like Kuya Jepoy said, people change.

But will it be too late for me?

"I don't want to die, Ate." I bite my lower lip. "I can't die yet. We haven't seen Dad in over a year. What if he doesn't want to see us anymore? Wendell says Dad missed us, but we haven't really talked to Dad himself—"

"He wants to see us." Ate Nadine says it with so much conviction, I feel like I need to believe her. "Dad has done everything he can to get better. For us, and for himself."

I lean against her side, resting my head on her shoulder. A smile forms on my lips. "So you're admitting that you're wrong about Dad, then."

"I didn't—" My sister gasps. She wiggles her index finger. "Hey! Are you sassing me?"

"Nooooooo!"

I cover my sides, protecting them from my sister's tickles.

But Ate Nadine is too fast. "You can't be Sab. The real Sab doesn't sass me. You're an alien taking over her body. Get out, alien! Bring back my baby sister."

We collapse on the grass in giggles. Ate Nadine doesn't stop her tickle attack until she has her arms around my shoulders, pinning me against her. We both gasp for breath, and before long, our laughter dies down.

I feel like the weight of the world is lifted off me. Whatever negativity that's been keeping us back is gone now. We'll be at the resort in no time.

Well, after Ate Nadine manages to change the tire, that is.

CHAPTER TWENTY-FIVE
Lola Cordia's Garden Resort

I THINK I MIGHT HAVE spoken too soon.

As we near the resort, Ate Nadine is gazing through the window. Worry lines stretch across her forehead, like she's anxiously awaiting feedback from her internship boss.

"Look, Ate!" I point at a group of little brown ducks foraging outside a restaurant. "It's Lawin's cousins."

"Lawin is a Pekin duck, sweetie," Mom says, chuckling. "Those are itik."

"I know that." I turn to Ate Nadine for support, waiting for her to argue how ducks are created equal regardless of breed. But she doesn't. It's like my sister doesn't even hear us, cooped up in her own world where no one exists but herself.

Tito Ed turns left to an unmarked road narrow enough for a single car. I've always wondered what would happen if there was another car coming from the opposite direction. Who would give way? What if they chance upon the part of the road where there's hardly enough space to pull over because of bamboo fences and banana trees?

As usual, we don't encounter any other vehicle that will give us this very problem. A year may have passed, but the road leading to the Dulce family resort remains as peaceful as it was before.

There isn't much to see except for trees, and maybe a house or two. Every now and then, we'll see laundry spread out on the side of the road or rice grains forming golden carpets while drying under the sun.

On our left, grass and coconut trees become high walls made of concrete and decorative stones. Tito Ed slows the SUV and stops beside a sign that says LOLA CORDIA'S GARDEN RESORT. The security guards see Mom in the passenger seat. They open the white gates and happily invite us in.

"Oh, good. Christopher took my advice and installed security cameras," Tito Ed says, nodding at the devices attached to the gate posts. "Human eyes can't see everything."

Mom lets out a snort similar to Ate Nadine's. "My bet is on Wendell. I doubt Christopher remembered anything you've said."

Pepper giggles, and I join in despite myself. Mom turns to face us, giving us a wink. Dad would forget to brush his teeth if Wendell didn't remind him. That's just who he is.

There's a crunching sound as Tito Ed brings the car inside the resort. I can't believe we're here! The gravel driveway is exactly as I remember. Long and winding, it has trees lining its sides, the branches forming a natural roof above it. At the end of the flowery tunnel is the reception house—a small cottage with colorful windows and glass doors.

The lot beside the lobby is already full with guest-owned vehicles, but the parking aide leads us to a paved road on the other side of the cottage. He removes the chain with a PRIVATE PROPERTY sign and waves us through.

Tito Ed drives down the steep, tree-lined road. He maneuvers the turns carefully to avoid life-sized sculptures displayed in the oddest places. He parks the SUV at a carport beside the main house, where we find two men waiting at the front porch.

One is tall, with a buzz cut and skin as light as Pepper's. The other man is shorter and has a ponytail and a goatee. He also has dark skin and a flat nose like me. Wendell and Dad.

Tito Ed kills the engine and joins Mom to greet them.

Lawin quacks and struggles in my arms, his claws scratching my legs. "Hey! Calm down."

"You need to get out, Ate Nadine." Pepper lifts her backpack. "We're all stuck here until you do."

"This isn't the only door." My sister sinks deeper in her seat. Honestly, I want to sink along with her. "There's one beside you."

"Can't. There's a gross puddle outside."

With the windows closed and the aircon turned off, it's starting to heat up like an oven in the car. I'm trembling, and my heart is beating faster than I can think, but I don't want to stay in here. "Ate, if you don't open the door, we'll all collapse like that lady on the MRT."

Luckily, I don't have to wait long. Ate Nadine holds her breath and exhales aloud. She repeats it a few more times—like she's doing breathing exercises—until finally, she opens the door.

By this time, Dad and Wendell have already reached the car. As soon as my sister steps out, Dad hugs her. "I've missed you," he says.

"Dad, I—"

"Shh." Dad gives Ate Nadine a kiss on the forehead. "Where's my birthday girl?"

"Here." I step out of the car and release Lawin from his cage. He runs straight for the grass and flowers beside the parking lot. "I have a duck."

"Yes. And your hair—it's so short!" Dad smiles, his arms wide open. Maybe Ate's right. Maybe Dad's changed. His hair is longer than since we last saw him a year ago at Lola Cordia's funeral. His shirt has some streaks of paint, but it's not the ratty T-shirt he's fond of wearing. Dad's cleaned up well, that's for sure.

Pepper gives me a push. "Go. Your papa's waiting."

I step into Dad's arms.

"You're getting heavy," Dad grunts as he lifts me off the ground. I can see the stubble on his chin and that lone pimple scar on his neck's otherwise flawless skin. He smells the same as I remember, like chocolate and peppermint and acrylic paint. "My big girl, Sab."

Wendell clears his throat. "Happy birthday, Sab."

Up close, Wendell looks the same as he had since Lola Cordia's funeral. Tall, fair-skinned, and sporting the same semi-bald haircut.

Dad puts me down and nods at his boyfriend.

Wendell and Ate Nadine are both staring at their feet. To my surprise, my sister offers her hand. Wendell ignores it and pulls her into a tight hug instead.

Dad joins them, and so do I.

From behind Ate Nadine, I see Mom dabbing her eyes with a napkin. Tito Ed seems like he's trying not to cry. Beside him, Pepper gives me the thumbs-up sign.

Dad and Ate Nadine have made peace at least. It's what I've been hoping for. But something is still missing, words still left unsaid. For now though, this is enough for me.

CHAPTER TWENTY-SIX
The Butterfly's Warning

AFTER SWIMMING, EVERYONE'S OUT DOING their own thing. Mom's reading a book by the pool with Tito Ed, who's on his second coffee as he flips through the morning's paper. Wendell and Ate Nadine are playing badminton a few yards away. Near them, Dad repairs the flamingo sculptures scattered in the garden. Lawin's napping in his crate, satisfied after gorging himself silly with sliced cucumbers and tomatoes.

The resort staff set up a table in the gazebo, and it's now littered with my art stuff. I'm still out of oil pastels, so I'm stuck with regular crayons.

"I wonder what we'll be having for your party," Pepper says, stuffing a peeled mango into her mouth.

"Really?" I color the areas within the outlines of my sketch yellow. "You haven't even finished lunch dessert yet."

"I'm a growing girl." Pepper takes another big bite of her mango. There's a squishy sound near my ear as she chews and looks over my shoulder. "Those are pretty sea stars."

"They're supposed to be ylang-ylang flowers." I rub the edges of the droopy petals to blend the colors, but nothing happens. Regular crayons don't work well for me. I toss the crayon on the table. "This isn't working."

"Don't. I'll keep it." Pepper takes the drawing before I can tear it up. "Mama loves your art, and so do I."

"Your friend's right. Those are beautiful flowers."

I look up and find Dad staring at my art. A wave of sadness washes over me. Dad used to help me a lot with my art when he wasn't cooped up in his studio. He even taught me how to use oil pastels, which became my favorite medium. Dad was always encouraging, even when my works were sometimes a flop.

Dad sits down beside me. He picks up a crayon and begins doing a quick sketch of a tree. An ylang-ylang tree. He pushes the drawing toward me. "Your turn. Color them yellow. Or green. Anything you like. You're only limited by your imagination, baby girl."

Soon Wendell and Tito Ed join us at the table. And I'm done with my art. It's better than the first version I made, that's for sure.

"Anybody up for a game of badminton?" Tito Ed waves around the rackets. "We can play doubles."

Ate Nadine shows up, sweaty from the game. She takes a glass of water and chugs it down. "Wendell's a beast with the racket."

"Me!" Pepper jumps off her seat. "Teach me how!"

"I'm done." Ate Nadine winces, slouching on a chair. She takes a mango and peels it as messily as Pepper did.

"No, thank you." I move my things away from my sister. Regular crayons may not be my best medium, but I don't like getting my stuff icky with mango juice.

"I'll just challenge the winner," Wendell says, smiling. "I need to check on the party preparation. Christopher, are you coming?"

Dad shakes his head.

Pepper chugs down water before following Tito Ed to the field. Wendell makes his way to the resort kitchen.

Alone with my father and Ate Nadine, we sit in silence as we avoid one another's gazes. It's uncomfortable, and it's weird. But it's a start, being at the same table together.

Dad gets up from his seat. "Can you girls come with me for a bit? There's something I'd like to show you."

I throw a look at my sister. She nods, and I stand at the same time she does.

"It's just something I'm working on," Dad says, his expression unreadable. "I think you'll like this."

Dad brings us to the main house, where we pass through the living room full of clocks and statuettes of the Child Jesus in varying shapes and sizes. We enter the hallway, where we see a life-sized painting of Dad's parents hanging on the wall. It shows my grandfather smiling through his white beard like a jolly Filipino Santa Claus. His big stomach hides behind an ornate chair, where Lola Cordia sits like a queen. Her expression reminds me of a jail warden having a bad day at the correctional facility.

The picture of Lola Cordia reminds me of a question I've been meaning to ask my father. Well, aside from the whole drug thing, that is. "Did Lola know about you and Wendell?"

Dad stops and stares at the artwork. He touches Lola Cordia's painted hand as though he's covering it with his own.

"I think she did. I never said anything, but I wish I did when I had the chance."

Lola Cordia's death took the doctors by surprise. She suffered an incredibly high level of blood sugar. Like, a you-can-die-any-minute-now kind of level. Then she got well. A week later, the doctor deemed her okay. But on that same night, she passed in her sleep.

I wonder if Dad saw the Butterfly before Lola Cordia died.

"Lola always liked Wendell. She said he was good for you," Ate Nadine says. I look twice to be certain she's the one speaking. "And I agree."

Dad's brows shoot to his forehead. I don't blame him.

I always had the impression that Lola Cordia might not have accepted Dad's identity. She was very religious—she liked things to be a certain way. They must be what she expected them to be, or she got upset.

"What? It's what Lola said." Ate Nadine shrugs. "So. Is this what you're going to show us, Dad?"

"Oh no. Not that." Dad opens the door to the patio, and we follow him through a pergola of climbing plants with bright pink flowers. The tunnel is quite like the driveway, but cozier and just wide enough for people to walk through.

Unlike roses, bougainvillea blooms don't have a strong scent. But the vines encasing the pathway are so closely knit we emerge to the pavilion smelling like foliage and wet from falling dewdrops.

Wind blows from the east, bringing along the familiar scent of ylang-ylang flowers. They look like slivers of dried mango strips hanging on the branches. A concrete sign saying BUTTERFLY GARDEN marks a path under the trees.

"You can see the butterflies later." Dad puts an arm around me, steering me back to the main walkway. "Wendell and I didn't know how to care for them as well as Mama Cordia did, so we just let them go. But they're still around. I guess they love the resort flowers."

Dad leads us farther to the edge of the property, where a small cottage stands hidden among the trees. Its stained glass windows are wide and colorful, letting sunlight in from every angle. He opens the door and we find ourselves inside his workshop.

Half-finished sculptures litter the floor, while completed ones are left on the table to dry. Dad takes a box from a cabinet, lifting an artwork from inside it.

I gasp and take a step back. My foot gets caught in a twisted rag on the floor, but Ate Nadine steadies me.

It's a sculpture of a butterfly. Bigger than my hand, this clay insect bears a striking resemblance to the one that foretold my future. Dad painted it in black but added a few touches of silver on its wings.

"I call this *The Butterfly's Warning*," Dad says, pushing the artwork to the middle of the table. His eyes are on me as he speaks, and I feel like I've lost the ability to breathe. "Do you recall those stories I told you about the Butterfly?"

Ate Nadine and I both nod.

"Wendell always said it's just a superstition. So did your mom," Dad continues. "But it's real."

Of course it is. I've seen it twice this week.

I remember that day Wendell called to check up on us, just before I saw the Butterfly. "Did you recently see the Butterfly, Daddy?"

Dad studies me before answering. Ate Nadine is tapping a finger on the table, like she's waiting for his answer too.

"No," he finally says, shaking his head. "I didn't."

Ate Nadine clears her throat. Dad and I turn our attention to her at the same time.

"Where do you think this Butterfly comes from?" she asks in a brisk manner. Ate Nadine's forehead is crunched up in concentration, and I can almost see the gears turning inside her head. It's as if her "journalist radar" has lit up.

"Mama said I saw what I saw because of my creativity. I'm naturally inclined to open my mind to external things, such as intuition about what is yet to come. It is also a symbol of change, you know." Dad clears his throat. He reaches for the sculpture and touches the clay butterfly's right wing. "For the past week, I got this feeling about you two. *Something's not right.* Wendell thought I'm just missing you girls. Thank goodness he's right."

It's too soon to say. After all, it's still morning. Besides, it was probably my bad thoughts about him that my dad was feeling.

But I keep my gloomy thoughts to myself. If I only have this day left with my family, I should make every minute count. To pretend the Butterfly doesn't exist is easier, but it's not the right thing to do.

I'm not blowing my chance to find the answers I seek. "Daddy."

"Yes, baby girl?"

I take a deep breath. *Here goes.* "Did you do drugs because you had Ate Nadine and me?" If he says yes, it'll break my heart. But I have to know. "Did you ever love us, Daddy?"

"Oh, baby girl." Dad reaches out to hug me, but I step back. A lump forms in my throat.

"No. Tell me, Daddy. I *need* to know!"

"I'm so sorry I made you feel that way. Mahal na mahal kita. I love you so, so much. It was never about you," Dad says, his lower lip quivering. Tears well up in my eyes when I notice his are getting wet too. "I'm not going to justify what I did—it was very wrong. I'll understand if you hate me for it, but please know I'm doing my best to stay clean. I don't want to hurt you all again."

"I forgive you," Ate Nadine says in a quiet voice. "I'm *trying* to forgive you. It's hard, but it's getting there."

Dad bites his lower lip as tears fall down his cheeks. My own tears follow suit.

It was a terrible, terrible thing he did. It tore apart our family. But he *is* my father.

"I love you, Daddy," I say, throwing my arms around my father's waist. I wish we had more time to go through the journey of healing together. This is something we should face as a family, but my time is about to run out. Maybe the angels in heaven will let me watch him and everyone I love from the clouds.

Dad hugs me back, while Ate Nadine strokes my hair.

"I love you too. I love you both." Dad pulls my sister in to join us. Ate Nadine doesn't protest, hugging both Dad and me.

I look up at Ate Nadine. The worry lines on her face have disappeared. No matter what happens next, at least my dad and sister have begun to work things out.

Finally, I'm at peace.

CHAPTER TWENTY-SEVEN
Tick-Tock, Goes the Clock

TICK-TOCK.

I sit between Pepper and Ate Nadine on the sofa, with Lawin sleeping on my lap. It's a tight fit, but it's the best place to watch all the clocks in the living room.

Tick-tock.

Amidst the different statuettes of the Child Jesus, there's a ceramic clock shaped like a birdhouse and another in the form of a plate. A metal timepiece is attached to the frame of Dad and Wendell's photo, while the one beside it is on the stomach of a plastic cat. The digital clock on the mantel displays not only hours and minutes but seconds as well.

Tick-tock.

The clocks come in different forms, but they all say the same:

It's one minute to five o'clock. One minute before I die.

Ate Nadine holds my hand tightly. Her skin is almost as cold as mine.

I wonder how I will die. Will I choke to death? Will I suddenly erupt in hives? Will the house collapse on my head?

Either way, I hope it'll be a painless death. It's the least Death can do for taking me from this world too soon.

I touch Lawin's feathered head. Maybe God will let me visit him from time to time as a ghost. I just hope I don't scare him too much.

My pulse quickens with every tick of the clock.

Five . . .

Four . . .

Three . . .

Two . . .

Ding-dong! Ding-dong!

The clocks chime at the same time, my heart thumping with every sound. They ring five times, then stop.

And I'm still alive.

"It's all over!" Pepper raises her arms in the air, whooping. Her sudden movement startles Lawin, who jumps off my lap and waddles around the living room in circles.

"Yes, it is." I can't believe it. I didn't die.

"You're okay." Ate Nadine pulls me in a tight hug. "We're all okay."

"We are," I mumble through her blouse. As usual, she smells like strawberries and cream. "Can't breathe."

"Sorry." Ate Nadine releases me, smiling sheepishly. Her eyes are wet with tears—happy tears. "Your drama is so contagious. It's your fault I'm crying."

I smile through my own tears. "Well, you *were* scared too."

"Of course I was. I'm your sister."

No, I'm not going to cry again. But my eyes seem to know better. I tear up once more. "Even though it means you're stuck with me longer?"

Ate Nadine pretends to think.

"Ate!"

"I'm kidding." Ate Nadine laughs. She reaches behind Pepper and me, tickling us. Our squeals turn to giggles, and soon enough, we're a tangled heap on the living room floor.

It's nice to feel silly again. No prophetic butterflies, no deaths to worry about. I don't have to wonder what my life would be like if I live past the age of eleven. Because now, I will. I'm not dying today.

CHAPTER TWENTY-EIGHT
The Black Butterfly

WENDELL REALLY KNOWS HOW TO throw a party.

Even with such short notice, he managed to fill the buffet table with all the dishes I love. He had the resort staff close the pavilion to customers, installing bamboo dividers all around. They hung strings of fairy lights from the center of the ceiling, creating a magical canopy over the dining tables with matching ornate chairs. The last rays of the sun turn the white tablecloths red-orange, and guests have begun to arrive.

I recognize a few faces—Dad's cousins, aunts, and uncles. A few have toddlers with them, while some have teens a bit younger than Ate Nadine. However, no niece or nephew seems to be around the same age as Pepper and me.

We don't mind. We're fine snacking on deep-fried corn kernels and garlic peanuts.

Well, that is until the kitchen staff brings out the lechon baboy. Pepper and I spring off our chairs like jack-in-the-boxes.

"It's so *beautiful*." Pepper sighs as we follow the roasted pig to the buffet table, where the servers ready it for chopping.

Yes, it is. My mouth waters at the thought of dipping the shiny, toasted cracklings in sweet liver sauce. I can't wait to dig in.

"Easy there, tigers. You'll have all the lechon you want later," Wendell's high-pitched voice chirps between Pepper and me. He leans down and puts an arm around my shoulders. "It's almost time to blow out your candles, Sab."

Pepper tears her eyes away from the roasted pig. "Doesn't candle-blowing happen when everyone's eaten? I want to eat!"

"Usually." Wendell grins. "But I'd rather get the program out of the way so everyone can eat uninterrupted. Better find your sister, Sab. Unless you want to blow out your candles without her?"

I shake my head. After everything that's happened, I'm not blowing out any candle without Nadine. "I know where she is."

Even at night, the butterfly garden is as enchanting as it is in daylight. Ylang-ylang trees surround the entire vicinity, and bushes of various flowers decorate the pebble paths. A small fountain with yellow lights flows in the middle of the garden, the trickle of water providing calm to even the most turbulent soul. Every now and then, a sleeping butterfly will flap its wings.

Ate Nadine and I used to go here all the time whenever we visited Lola Cordia. Our grandmother loved those insects. It's too bad Dad couldn't take care of them.

But he's right. The butterflies just couldn't stay away.

I find Ate Nadine sitting on Lola Cordia's favorite bench, the one beside a retro lamppost. She's staring at the sky. "I asked for a new assignment at my internship today. I'm not doing news anymore."

"What?" My jaw drops. "Why?"

"Come sit with me," she says, patting the space on the bench beside her. As soon as I join her, she puts an arm around my shoulders. "I wasn't sure if I did the right thing, so I came here. Lola Cordia said the butterflies gave her peace, and she was right."

"But Dad said Lola's the one who told him that black butterflies bring death."

"Yeah." Ate Nadine gestures at a cluster of sleeping butterflies by the fountain. "Those aren't black, are they?"

Good point.

"But that website said—"

"—they're souls of the dead," Ate Nadine finishes for me, rolling her eyes. "I know, Sab. You left your browser window open on Mom's computer."

"I swear I saw the Butterfly, Ate."

"I believe you," she says, turning to smile at me. "I may not see it like you do, but it's important to you. Besides, there are just some things we won't be able to explain as simple as black and white. Real or not real."

I notice Ate Nadine still hasn't answered my question. "Why don't you want to be in the news section anymore, Ate? Isn't it your dream to be a journalist? Is it because of what happened in the alley?"

Ate Nadine winces. I regret my question instantly.

Of course my sister feels bad about what happened. No one died, but shots were fired and Kuya Jepoy got arrested for something he didn't do. If the rumors are true, people were put in danger because of Ate Nadine's report. And I just foolishly reminded her of it. "I'm sorry."

My sister just continues to stare at the night sky. It takes a few agonizing minutes before she finally speaks. "It's still my dream," she says. "And I'm still a journalist. But I'm going to do a different thing now. More reflective, more investigative. Not just straight-out news. I feel it's not enough to just tell what's happening. I need to take a stand too." Ate Nadine smiles. "I'm lucky my boss is good with that. And there's one more thing."

"What?"

"I asked for a short break. I'll be very busy again when school starts in June, so I want to spend at least a week of summer with you." Ate Nadine playfully tugs my hair. "Didn't you say you wanted to go to that water park in Laguna?"

My eyes grow wide. "For real?"

"For real."

I squeal and hug my sister in delight. "Oh, I love you!"

"I love you too, kiddo." Ate Nadine laughs, but the happy sound dies down. She gently disentangles herself from my embrace, turning to face me. "This thing about dealing with Dad's addiction . . . We're only just beginning. I've talked to Mom, Tito Ed, Wendell, and even Dad. We figured it's about time we go into counseling and work things out as a family, so we can start to heal. Are you okay with that?"

The mere thought of facing all those years of hurt scares me, but I trust Ate Nadine. "Okay."

"I'm going to be with you every step of the way. We're in this together. You have nothing to worry about—"

"I know, Ate." I didn't understand it before, but I do now. As a lone butterfly flutters up to join a cluster on top of the fountain, an idea occurs to me. "Do you think the black butterfly I saw . . ." I pause. "Do you think that was Lola Cordia? Like, maybe she wanted things to get better for us."

Ate Nadine tilts her head. "I wouldn't be surprised if she did."

I think back to the things I've learned this week. From the people I've met, the places I've been, to the stories I've uncovered about my family. Especially with my dad.

I got my heart broken, and it's still mending. Yet, the more I think about it, the more I realize it's not as terrible as I thought.

Those truths showed me that Dad's human too—he made mistakes like any other person. His bad choices had grave consequences, but he's trying his best to make up for it. I'll never look at him the same way again, and that's okay.

I still love Dad. Perhaps even more so now, knowing that he isn't perfect. Same with Ate Nadine.

A warm breeze touches the back of my neck, while goose bumps appear on my arms. The air smells like ylang-ylang flowers. I look up, and so does Ate Nadine. It's like we're drawn to it somehow. The black butterfly.

It flutters down and lands on my forehead, but only for a second—like a kiss. It's just like the way our lola liked to kiss us when she was still alive.

"Lola Cordia?" I whisper.

A tear slides down Ate Nadine's cheek, touching that small smile on her lips. The butterfly flies into the light of the lamppost, vanishing before it reaches the top.

Ate Nadine puts her arm around me, and I rest my head on my sister's shoulder. Even in death, Lola Cordia sends me a birthday gift—the love of my sister, my dad, my family.

It's the best birthday gift ever.

"We should go back to your party," Ate Nadine suggests. "Your guests are waiting."

I take one last look at the place where the Butterfly disappeared. I'll have many more birthdays to come, but a girl turns eleven only once, after all. "Okay, Ate. Let's go."

Author's Note

A lot of things in this book are based on real life but were fictionalized to fit a story that mixes reality, magic, and everything in between.

Even though I reside outside of Metro Manila now, I was born and raised in Quezon City like Sab. My dad is a photo journalist, and it was his love for sports, politics, and current events that inspired me to write for my school paper in college (just like Nadine).

It was my lola who first told me of the common Filipino belief that the appearance of a black butterfly means someone close to you has died. The funny thing is, she also said it wasn't real. But it didn't stop me from believing in it.

I believed I saw a black butterfly after my lola's sister died. I saw one after a friend expired. And I was certain I saw one after my lola herself passed away. I would see these butterflies for only a few seconds, then they seemingly disappeared in mid-flight.

It may simply be a coincidence, seeing a butterfly just hours before getting the news of loved one's death. Perhaps Pepper's right that these butterflies simply made their way in from the garden. Maybe I just imagined the black butterflies. Or maybe this magic is real.

Maybe. Maybe not.

Either way, I hope this story based on the Filipino superstition of the black butterfly will give everyone a glimpse of my culture.

I also wished to write a story that would be a mirror for anyone who sees themself in Sab.

I'm brown and flat-nosed. Someone who looked like me was never the heroine in the books I read as a young girl. And as Nadine explained, colonial mentality is a reality in our culture—it made the lack of representation worse for me. So I promised myself I would one day write a book about Filipinos.

I did, and I hope that if you're like Sab and me, you'll remember that you don't need a light complexion and a high-bridged nose to be considered beautiful. Because you *are* beautiful.

People's assumptions are not always right. Sab assumed that someone like Jepoy was probably trouble—and that was also the assumption the cops made when they arrested him. But Jepoy was drug free. It was Sab's own middle-class dad who had an addiction problem.

There are times when incorrect assumptions can take a deadly turn, like what happened to a seventeen-year-old student named Kian Loyd delos Santos in Metro Manila in 2017.

Similar to Jepoy, Kian was suspected of being involved in illegal drugs. But he wasn't as fortunate. Kian was shot by the police.

They claimed he resisted arrest, but witnesses and CCTV footage said otherwise.

Kian's death became the subject of a Senate hearing, eventually resulting in stricter guidelines in the implementation of Operation Tokhang. On November 29, 2018, the Caloocan Regional Trial Court Branch 125 found the three cops involved guilty of his murder. Still, Kian's death and thousands of others remain a bloody footprint in this war on drugs.

Kian died because of wrong assumptions, just because he fit the "profile" of a drug runner—a teenage boy from a low economic class.

Drug addiction is a reality that a lot of families—rich and poor—grapple with, both here in the Philippines and around the world.

If someone close to you is suffering from addiction, keep in mind that it's not your fault. Addiction is a disease that is out of your control. As Sab's mom said, this disease makes people do mean and silly stuff they wouldn't do if they weren't using. But that doesn't make them bad people. They have a disease and they deserve help.

So do you.

Seek help from your elders. Reach out to your family and friends. It's totally okay to talk about the problem. Remember, recovery is not just about your addicted loved one getting rehabilitation. Everyone in the family should get support too—and that includes you. Recovery is a long journey for the whole family to find peace and healing.

You can also visit these websites for more information about addiction and where to find help:

NACoA, or the National Association for Children of Alcoholics (*nacoa.org*), is an organization dedicated to help children with parents addicted to drugs or alcohol. They have a kit especially made for you that you can download from their website: *nacoa.org/resource/kit-for-kids/*

Al-Anon Family Groups offer support for the loved ones of addicts and alcoholics. *al-anon.org*

The **American Addiction Centers** website has a comprehensive guide for children of addicted parents. *americanaddictioncenters.org/guide-for-children*

NCTSN, or the National Child Traumatic Stress Network, provides a database of resources for children dealing with traumatic experiences. *nctsn.org/resources*

For Philippines-based readers, remember the pink-and-purple building Sab mentioned in the book? It was based on an actual facility in Pasig City, the **Metro Psych Facility: Roads and Bridges to Recovery:** *metropsych.net*. They also have a rehabilitation center in Cebu.

You don't have to go through this on your own. You are not alone.

Acknowledgments

People say writing is a solitary art. Well, maybe the actual act of writing is, but this book wouldn't be a book without the support and generosity of so many people.

I'm grateful for the kindhearted souls I subjected to reading early versions of my story: Elena Jagar, Akossiwa Ketoglo, Jessi Cole Jackson, Greg Andree, Maria Frazer, and Cla Ines. Your feedback meant the world to me. And thank you, Sarah Kettles and Joy McCullough, for helping me prepare for the querying trenches.

Without the guidance of my amazing mentors, my Writing Ates—Erin Entrada Kelly, Kate Messner, and Anica Mrose Ricci—my publishing journey would have taken so much longer. I can't thank you enough for helping me become the writer I never thought I could be. And of course, many thanks to Justina Ireland for letting me be part of Writing in the Margins. To say your mentoring program changed my life would be an understatement.

My Scholastic family, who worked tirelessly to bring Sab's story into the hands of kids everywhere—you have my utmost gratitude. Special thanks to Amy Goppert for helping me get the word out about my book, to Oriol Vidal for giving me the very Filipino book cover of my dreams, to Baily Crawford for the gorgeous book design, and to copyeditor Jessica Rozler and production editor Josh Berlowitz for their care and sensitivity. I'm so lucky to have worked with such a talented and hardworking team!

An infinity of thanks to my editor, Emily Seife, who took a chance with Sab and me. Your editing skills are nothing short of magic, turning my caterpillar of a manuscript into a beautiful butterfly—a colorful butterfly, not the scary kind.

I will forever be grateful to my agent, Alyssa Eisner Henkin, my fearless champion and sounding board, who has miraculously turned my "I cannot" into "I can." Thank you for your faith in me, and for believing my stories full of Filipino quirks are worth sharing with the rest of the world.

I'd be lost without my girls: Rin Chupeco, Kara Bodegón, Hazel Ureta, Tarie Sabido, Alechia Dow, and Elsie Chapman. Your friendship, solidarity, and writerly talks make writing less lonely than it should be. Same goes for my Write Pack—KC Johnson, Ronni Selzer, Ely Azure, and Rena Barron—you ladies rock.

My space princess, Rae Somer, and my Filipino mermaid, Isabelle Adrid, you two are the Pepper to my Sab. Thank you,

Eloisa San Juan and Nina Fuentes, for accompanying me on food trips across Metro Manila whenever I needed a writing break.

Many, many thanks to my parents, August and Jocelyn, who have always supported my book obsession and encouraged my writing (and even the strangest of my hobbies). And to my younger sister, Joyce, who has been my number one fan since forever. I couldn't ask for a more supportive family. Everything I am, everything I will be, is because of you.

To Marc, my husband, my best friend, and the love of my life: Thank you for putting up with my wild ideas, for making sure I don't starve whenever I'm on a deadline, for driving me to places I need or want to be, for keeping my feet on the ground. I don't know what I'd do without you and your unwavering love and support. I love you, forever and ever.

Last but not the least, thank you to my lola in heaven. I wrote a book, Mama Nena. I never would have been able to if you hadn't patiently taught me to read. I hope I made you proud.

About the Author

Gail D. Villanueva is a Filipino author born and based in the Philippines. She's also a web designer, an entrepreneur, and a graphic artist. She loves pineapple pizza, seafood, and chocolate, but not in a single dish together (ewww). Gail and her husband live in the outskirts of Manila with their dogs, ducks, turtles, cats, and one friendly but lonesome chicken. Learn more at gaildvillanueva.com.